The Willow

and other tales

Robert A Lane

Pen Press

TO
MAGGIE
HOPE YOU LIKE
MY LATEST
STORY BOOK
YOUR
FRIEND
ROBERT A

First published in Great Britain by Pen Press

All paper used in the printing of this book has been made from wood grown in managed, sustainable forests.

ISBN13: 978-1-907172-35-9

Printed and bound in the UK
Pen Press is an imprint of Indepenpress Publishing Limited
25 Eastern Place
Brighton
BN2 1GJ

A catalogue record of this book is available from the British Library

Cover design by Jacqueline Abromeit

Contents

Dedication

To my very close and good friend
Sara Bond
for without her help this book would
never have gone to print

Part One

The Clock That Did Not Chime

I've got a funny story to tell you, or should I say a strange one. It was in 1979 and we went to Portsmouth to go on the Old Victory – Lord Nelson's ship. We went on the ship and had a good day out. It was only two o'clock and our hotel was close to the dock so we took a slow walk back passing lots of little shops, which we looked in as we went. There was an old junk shop that could have done with a lick of paint and the window was full…you name it and it was there. I didn't say anything to Harry but I could feel myself being drawn in.

The next day we went shopping and again found ourselves looking in the junk shop window. I noticed that there were new things there and yet again, the day after, when we had been on a boat trip, something was telling me to go back to the shop. So, I told Harry that there was a seafood café near the shop and we made our way there and for the third time we stopped outside the junk shop and looked in the window. This time my eyes went straight to an old mantelpiece clock with a price tag of £15. The bottom of the clock was square, the face was round with big black numbers and hanging by a string was a big winged key. It was a good size clock – about 18 inches high – and I was so taken with it that I went into the shop and asked about it. The assistant took it out of the window and told me that it was a 7-day wind-up clock that chimed on the hour. "It was made in Birmingham in 1916 by Samuell Berklen Ltd," he said. "Sadly it doesn't work – give me £10 and it's yours."

Harry bought me the clock and we went off to the seafood café. Harry said the food was the best seafood he had eaten in years and I told him about how something had kept drawing me back to the junk shop.

"I know," he'd said to me. "You don't stay married for someone for so long without getting to know their ways. I knew that you hadn't found whatever it was you were looking for and then I knew, by the way you were looking at the clock, that it was that you had been looking for. Mind you, I am not complaining – we will be coming back here to eat again!"

Back at the hotel we gave the clock a good look over and found at the back a small door just big enough for a small hand to get in. Harry shone a torch inside and said he could see a piece of paper rolled up and pushed behind the chimes. So, using tweezers, he got it out and found it was a letter from a man named Tom to a lady called Sally.

Before I read the letter to you I want to go back to 1935, where the story starts.

The clock belonged to Tom's mother who died in 1935 and the clock was packed away until 1939 when Tom found it. Tom Rain was his full name and he still lived in his mother's house, which she had left to him in her will.

In 1940 England was at war with Germany and Tom received his call-up papers to go into the army. His girlfriend was Sally Barns who loved him very much, just as he loved her. Tom put the clock on his mantelpiece. What Tom and Sally loved about the clock was that it chimed every hour. Sally was always on to Tom to give her the clock so that it would always remind her of him.

Sally's father did not like Tom – he thought Tom wasn't good enough for his daughter and she was only just 17, which was too young to go out with boys. Plus there was a war on and he could get killed. Sally's father was not a nice man and did not have many friends. He told her she was not to see Tom any more.

Sally told Tom that one day she would marry him and he asked her to wait for him until he came back from the war. Even though he could not see her he said he would write to her every week. Sally never got any letters from Tom as her father waited for the post and burnt all Tom's letters. This went on for five weeks until Tom had to go into the army. Then he wrote her a letter asking her to marry him when he returned, telling her he loved her very much and asking why she was not answering any of his letters, little knowing she never got any of them. He hid the letter inside the clock, pushing it against the chimes so that the clock could not chime on the hour. Knowing how much she loved the chimes she would open the back to see why and find his letter. He had the clock sent to her house and then went off to war.

When Sally got the clock she was so upset not hearing from him that she thought it was a goodbye present and that he did not love her anymore, so she just left it in the box and put it under her bed, and there it stayed.

While he was away in France and other countries he wrote to her every time he could get a letter posted home, but still Sally's father burnt them. Sally still loved Tom and she knew she always would but while the war was on her father got boys to call on her, and she went out with a few. One was a boy called Martin but she saw him only to get out of the house and away from her father (her mother had run off with a shoemaker when Sally was just a baby and a nanny had brought her up). Sally hated her father, so in 1944, after going out with Martin for nearly three years, he asked her to marry him. Although she did not love him he was good to her, he was kind and understanding, so Sally told Martin she was very fond of him but did not love him. All he said was, "I love you, let me look after you and one day you may grow to love me." So they married and moved up North where Martin had been offered a good job. In 1945 Sally's father died. Sally had not seen her father from the day she got married to the day he died. In his will he left the house to her and a letter but she would not open it and put it in the box with the clock.

Sally had a baby boy and girl and she gave Martin a good marriage – he was very happy with his life. But in 1960, Martin got caught in a heavy downpour; he was only wearing a pair of jeans and a shirt, caught pneumonia and a month later he died.

Sally had made lots of friends and one such friend had just moved to Portsmouth. She wrote to Sally saying, "Why don't you move down here? You've got the sea, lots of fresh air… it will be good for you all and there are lots of jobs." So Sally moved to Portsmouth and loved it straight away, and so did the children. She bought a little house, got a job and was very happy and her friend was always popping in for a chat.

Tom had spent all his time in the army abroad, writing to Sally whenever a letter could be sent home. He never got back to England until January 1946 and as soon as he did he went to Sally's house, but it was empty. The neighbours told him Sally had married a chap called Martin Bell and had moved up North. They told him that Sally's father had died in March 1945 and they did not know where she had moved to, nor did they have any forwarding address. Tom was sick inside that she did not wait for him and he thought she did not love him, which was why she had not answered any of his letters.

Tom went back to his mother's house and went out with lots of girls. He liked one girl called Peggy and after two years together they got married in 1951 – but he did not love Peggy, it was still Sally that he loved. Tom had one son but by 1964 his marriage was on the rocks and they divorced in 1965. His son went with his mother but was always popping in to see his dad and staying weekends as he loved his dad and Tom loved his son very much.

Now, let's go back to Harry and the letter he found rolled up inside the clock. It was from Tom to Sally dated April 7th 1940, with Tom's address. The letter started…

My Darling Sally,

Why have you not answered my letters? I have written to you every week. I have to go into the Army on the 21st April and I don't know how long the war will last or how long I will be away, or if I will come back home. If I do and when it's all over I will ask you to marry me for I love and miss you very much. I know you always wanted the clock so it's yours, my darling. Think of me now and then, I will write to you while I am away.

My love is only for you for all time.

I love you my darling.

Tom xxxx

Harry said, "How long ago did Tom write this letter?"

"1940," I replied. "It's now 1978, that's 38 years of age. What shall we do Harry?"

"When we go home let's drive to where Tom lived or still lives – I know Mordon, south-west London. Let's hear the chimes."

We both agreed the chimes were lovely to listen to. On the following Monday we drove over to Mordon and luck was with us for we got to Tom's house at two o'clock and knocked on the door. A man opened the door, he was about 60 years old, a good-looking, big man, healthy looking, softly spoken.

"Can I help you," he asked.

"Are you Tom Rain?" enquired Harry.

"Yes, why do you ask?"

"Could we come in? My name is Harry Morgan and this is my wife Jean. We have a clock we want to ask you about."

"Yes come in please, now what's this about a clock?"

I took the clock out of my bag and Tom could not speak, he just looked at the clock. Eventually Tom asked, "Where did you get this clock?"

"We got it from a junk shop," Harry replied.

"Where?"

"In Portsmouth. Is this clock yours?"

"Yes but I gave it to a girl called Sally. I loved her and wanted to marry her after the war but she married a man called Martin and moved up North. I have never seen or heard from her since 1940."

"Yes we know"

"You know, but how do you know?"

"I will tell you in a minute. The chimes work on the clock now – do you want to listen to them?"

We listened to the chimes and they brought tears to Tom's eyes

"One of the reasons we are here is to give you your clock back," said Harry, "And the second reason we are here is to give you back your letter."

As Harry gave Tom his letter Tom's eyes welled up again. "Thank you both for the clock and letter. I don't know of anyone who would do what you've done for me."

"Well," said Harry, "as long as you are happy we are happy."

We got up to leave and Tom thanked us both again. As we turned to go, Harry said, "You never know, we might meet again."

"You are always welcome to call in if you are passing," said Tom.

"What now Harry," I asked.

"Well tomorrow we go to Portsmouth, back to the junk shop," said Harry.

The next day we returned to the junk shop and I asked the shop owner if he remembered us.

"Yes of course, you bought the old 7-day clock, what can I sell you this time?"

"What we would like is the name of the lady who sold you the clock," said Harry.

"Why?" he asked.

So we told the shopkeeper what we hoped to do.

"Her name's Sally," said the shopkeeper. "I know her very well, she lives at Brown Fern House, 27 Bornfield Road, Portsmouth, Hants, and if I can help in any way please ring me."

Back home Harry rang his friend Norris, who worked in partnership as a solicitor at Norris and Bernard Coleman solicitors, asking for his help to bring two people together after 38 years. His friend said that if he could help Harry he would. Then Harry rang Tom and asked if I could borrow his clock for a few days, as I wanted to photograph it for my photography club. Tom agreed and dropped the clock over the very next day. I thanked him and said that as soon as I had taken the photos the clock would be returned.

A few days later Mrs Sally Bell got a letter from a solicitor asking her to call at his office in Ilford, Essex. "I can assure you that you need not worry, it is in your best interest," said the solicitor. "Can you be at our office on 24th July 1978 at 2.45pm, sharp, please, as it is important to you and to us. I will send the details with a map enclosed. Could you please phone us to let us know you can attend."

Sally rang the office and said that she would be there at the said time and date. At the same time Tom got a letter asking him if he could be at the same office in Ilford, Essex on 24th July 1978 at 2.45pm sharp, also asking him to call the office and confirm that he could attend.

On the 24th July Harry and I were at the solicitors waiting expectantly. At 2.45pm on the dot Sally walked into the office and was led to a small room to the left and was given a cup of tea. At 2.55pm Tom walked in and was taken to a small room to the right of the office, then the clock was bought out and put on the table in the waiting room next to the two rooms that Tom and Sally were in.

At three o'clock sharp the clock struck then the chimes started to play, and as soon as Tom heard the clock he jumped up and came out of his small room. As soon as Sally heard the chimes play she also jumped up, and ran out of her small waiting room. There, standing by the clock, stood a man who she recognised straight away and as soon as Tom saw her, he knew who she was.

They stood looking at each other and Sally said "Tom, Tom…" and Tom said "Sally, Sally…" and with that Sally ran to him throwing her arms around him and cried her eyes out, as Tom broke down and cried.

A while later Harry and I and Norris and Bernard came out of the office with a bottle of good wine. Sally said to Tom, "Why did you not write to me?"

"But I did, every week," said Tom.

"My father," said Sally. "He must have burnt the letters – I once saw a letter burning in the fire."

"Why did you not find out why the chimes in the clock didn't work?" asked Tom.

"Because I was upset with you for not writing. I thought you didn't love me anymore, that's why I married Martin. I told him I did not love him be he still wanted to marry me," Sally replied.

Tom informed Sally that the same thing had happened to him – he didn't think that Sally loved him anymore when he never got a letter, but that he'd always loved Sally and still did. Tom looked at Sally and said, "Will you marry me?"

"Yes, yes I will," Sally replied and started to cry again.

"Wait you two, I've got some money for you both," I said. "The photographs I took of your clock won me £100 in a competition so I've got £30 for each of you."

"No we can't take it," said both Sally and Tom, but I insisted saying, "You must, for the clock bought you together so please take it."

"Thank you all for what you have done for Tom and me," said Sally, "and you must all come to our wedding."

Tom and Sally got married on 26th September 1978. Tom sold his house and moved down to Portsmouth where they bought a big house. Tom's son left his mother and went to live with Tom, Sally and Sally's children, Ben and Carol, and they all lived very happily together.

At their wedding, Norris asked Harry and I how we knew about the clock.

"I didn't know about the clock," replied Harry.

"Well how did it all start?" asked Norris.

Harry told Norris that I have over 100 clocks from all over the world, all shapes, sizes and colours. I have this strange power to do with clocks and find ones that no one else will look at. The clock itself called out for help and, as only I can, I pick up the vibes.

Sally did open her father's letter that he left her on his deathbed. It said he was sorry for all the pain he had caused and that he had burnt all her letters and all Tom's letters. He knew he was wrong in what he had done and would she forgive him so that he could rest in peace. Sally had just three words for her father – "Go to hell!" Then she burnt his letter. It took Sally nearly 40 years to even the score but she felt it was worth the wait.

So the next time you see an old clock in a shop window, just think "I wonder if…"

The Big Old Teapot

The story I am going to tell you is one that I am unsure is true, for it goes back to the 1840s. My grandmother told me this story.

In 1840, in a small village called Lee Log lived a 56-year-old lady known as the 'rabbit lady'. Her real name was Mrs Lilac Thornby and she lived with her son Tommus. Together they made a living catching rabbits and selling them to anyone who wanted one. Whatever Mrs Thornby caught, she sold. Tommus went out and set the traps, he caught the rabbits and took them home to his mother who would sell them either in the market or door-to-door. Most nights Tommus would catch between three and seven rabbits but on a good night he could catch up to ten.

One day Lilac had sold all of her rabbits when a man came up to her and said, "I know a very, very old lady who cannot leave her cottage as she has hurt her leg. Will you take two of your rabbits to her the next time you have some? She lives in Little Bee Lane, right at the end, and she will pay you well."

The next day Lilac Thornby kept two big rabbits back and when she had sold the rest she took her horse and cart and went over to Little Bee Lane. Now, Lilac had been to Little Bee Lane many times before but she did not remember a cottage at the end of the lane. When she arrived she did indeed see a small cottage in front of her surrounded by a field with a large duck pond. In fact, all Lilac could see was fields, full of sheep, cows and horses – it looked different but it had been over two years since she had visited Little Bee Lane. Lilac walked to the cottage, knocked and waited. She knocked again and waited and was just about to return to her horse and cart when the door opened and a little old lady with a funny stick was stood in front of her. "I have brought you some rabbits" said Lilac.

"Yes," replied the old lady, "come in, come in…sorry you had to wait."

Inside, the cottage was spotless, everything was polished and there was lots of brass and a big fireplace. There was a huge oak table with four chairs and a big oil lamp sitting on top. Giving the rabbits to the old lady, Lilac informed her she had done well that day and was giving her the rabbits for free and then she asked her name.

"I am Mrs May Bell. I know they call you the rabbit lady but what is your name?"

"I am Mrs Lilac Thornby."

And so they began a conversation that lasted for almost an hour and Lilac made tea for them both before it was time for her to leave. "Listen," said Mrs Bell "as you will not let me pay you for the rabbits, I have a gift for you. It is a large, old teapot. I never use it and I would like you to have it. It was part of a special set with a cup, saucer and a cake plate but over the years these have got broken. I used to use it when friends called but now they have all gone. Then I then used it to keep money in but now I do not need money and so it just sits on the shelf. Please take it for me; you can use it if friends call, or you can use it to put your rabbit money in – it is a good hiding place. Now, remember what I tell you, once you have put a coin in this teapot there will always be money there, money to pay any bills that come your way. But you must never tell anyone that you hide your money in it – nobody, not even your son, because if you cheat the teapot you will regret it until your dying day."

With that, the old lady gave Lilac the teapot and bid her goodbye saying, "Remember my words."

The rabbit lady went home, not telling Tommus anything, and when, a few days later, she had one rabbit she hadn't sold she took it back up to Little Bee Lane to give to Mrs May Bell. However, when she got to the end of the lane there was no cottage. There were the same fields and the same duck pond but there was no little cottage. Lilac made her way back home, selling the rabbit on her way, and taking the money, she put it in the big old teapot as she had done every day since she had been given it.

Two months later the rabbit lady's horse died. Now, at that time horses were hard to get and very expensive but Lilac needed a horse in order to make a living. In the next village there was a horse for sale, which was exactly what she wanted. So Lilac told the horse seller that she wanted to buy it and asked how much it would cost. The man told her the price and Lilac said, "I will come back with the money tomorrow. If I am not back by tomorrow midday, please sell the horse for it means I have not found the money," to which the horse trader agreed.

On the way home Lilac said to her son, "I think I may have to borrow from you, for we need that horse, but I will know how much money I have when we get home."

Lilac waited until that evening when Tommus had gone to set the rabbit traps and then she emptied the teapot. Inside she found enough money to buy the horse and still have a few coins left over. She counted the money once, twice, three times, telling herself it couldn't be true – they surely hadn't sold enough rabbits to have all of this money in the teapot! Lilac did not tell Tommus that she had enough money; instead she borrowed from him and promised to pay him back as soon as she had sold enough rabbits. The next day Lilac went over to the village of Lee Field where she bought the horse and a month later she had paid her son back his money, still not telling him about the teapot. However, three months after this the wheels fell off her cart. Lilac now had a strong new horse but no cart for it to pull and without a cart, she could not work. Once again Lilac asked to borrow from Tommus so she could purchase a new one. Lilac went to the teapot and counted the money that was inside. Again she counted it once, twice, three times, and wondered once more how she had so much money. However, she had seen a strong new cart for sale in the village blacksmith yard and she had enough to buy it. Telling Tommus that she would pay him back a bit every day, Lilac went and bought the big new cart and so now with a strong new horse and a brand new cart she could find lots of work besides the rabbit money.

But there was one thing that she could not understand – it was something that the old lady had said to her. "Remember what I tell you, for this teapot will now be a part of your life," she had said, before adding…

> What you are to the teapot
> So shall the teapot be to you
> Your heart will ache
> The pot will break
> For greediness you did make
> This tree will end thee

No matter how many times she went over it, the proverb did not make any sense to her. She wrote it down and put it in the teapot and she still never spoke a word about it to her son.

Tommus had a nickname in the village – he was called 'Catch me Tommus' for when in the village tavern he would often talk about the rabbits that got away but he was really the best of the rabbit men for miles around and he was a good man with many friends. Tommus had seen the teapot at home many times but he had no idea where it had come from. All his mother had told him was that someone had given it to her, she had liked it so she had kept it. "But I don't want you to touch it in case you break it," she had said.

Tommus had looked at his mother and laughed. "Mother, mother," he had replied "Don't worry, I will not touch your teapot," and off he went to catch his rabbits.

For the next six months Lilac Thornby made a lot of money with her new big cart and her new young, strong horse. Because she could move heavier loads she was earning twice as much as before and this was separate from the money she made selling rabbits every day.

One day Tommus met a girl in another village and he wanted to marry her. It happened that on another occasion Lilac saw a beautiful big cottage for sale in another village and although it was a lot of money, she was sure that she might have enough in the teapot. Lilac went to look at the cottage and fell in love with it – she told the seller that she wanted it but needed to see if she had the money. "Come back tomorrow," the seller had said, "tell me yes or no as there are other people who want to look and to buy." So Lilac went straight home and looked in the teapot. The rabbit lady counted her money once, twice, three times and there was indeed enough to buy the cottage with some coins left over.

Tommus was away working for the girl he wanted to marry, on her father's land, so Lilac could not talk to him about the new cottage. Instead she bought it and moved her furniture into it before her son came home. When Tommus returned his mother told him, "You are a good son to me. Many times you have given me money, food and a share of the rabbits you have caught. So, as a wedding gift, I give you this cottage. It was your father's, then mine and now it is yours. You have more than paid for it, this is your bride-to-be's new home."

"Thank you, Mother," Ben replied. "I am your son and I want to make sure that you are ok with money and food. But as you say, with my help you are now fine and you have a new horse and cart and a new cottage to live in. Let's not speak of money again." From that day onwards mother and son never talked of money again.

Eight months later, at an old barn, some furniture was being sold at a very low price and Lilac wondered if she had enough in the teapot to buy. The seller told her she could give him part of the money immediately and pay the rest over time as he knew her and knew that she would pay him what she owed. The seller let her pick what she wanted and once she got home she emptied the teapot. Once more she counted the money once, twice, three times and found there was enough to pay for the furniture in full. So she went over to the seller, paid him and took all of her new furniture on her cart back to her new cottage. That night Lilac sat and tried to work out how, after taking all of the money out of the teapot, there were some coins left over. She knew that she had not added any more – had her son put money in the teapot for her? Had he found out where she kept her money? What a good son she had, he knew that she needed furniture for her new cottage. But how had he found it? Lilac had hidden it away – was it some sort of magic teapot? Whatever amount of money she wanted, she went to the teapot and it was there. "Don't be so silly," she told herself, "whoever heard of a magic teapot that gives you money whenever you want it." The old lady who had given it to her suddenly came into her mind. The day she had taken Mrs Bell the rabbits she was there in her little cottage at the end of the lane but when she went back the cottage was not there, only the fields and the duck pond. Since the old lady had given her the teapot she had acquired a new horse and cart, a bigger cottage and lots of new furniture and she had been able to leave her son the old cottage. "Everything is going well for me," she said to herself. "If the teapot is magic I can be a rich woman, for I only need to say I need money for this or for that and I will go to it and the money will be waiting for me. No! This is a silly thing to think. I work seven days a week and I work a long day, I earn my money and some days I put everything I have into the teapot – it must build up over the weeks and I have just not realised how much money

I have put away." "That must be the answer," she told herself. But that night she kept thinking – should she try and see if it was a magic teapot?

The next day Lilac went to look at another horse and cart that the blacksmith had for sale and again she made a deal and looked for a cart man to work them. She told a man who was looking for work to come to her cottage the following day and she would let him know if the job was his. Back home she went to the teapot and counted the money once, twice, three times and yes, there was enough money to buy the horse and cart and employ the cart man. But Lilac had not put any more money in the pot and so she realised, "I don't have to put any money into the pot – all I have to do is see something I want, look in the teapot and the money will be there." And this is what she did every time and every time the money was indeed there.

After a year of living in her new cottage the work started to dry up and Lilac had to lay off the cart man. At this point she was lucky if she got three days' work a week but every time she wanted money the teapot gave it to her. So Lilac started to go to the village tavern, drinking a few ales to start with and then slowly more and more. She was spending money like water. She slept all day and never went out to look for work as she just took more and more from the pot.

One night in the tavern Lilac was drunk and she made a bet on a horse called 'Daylight' who won the race making her a lot of money, which, instead of putting away, she gambled and bought drinks.. There came to be a very big county horse race and again Lilac was drunk in the village tavern and she wanted to place a bet on a horse called 'Gipsy Teapot' who was the favourite to win. However, she had run out of money and was not allowed to bet. "I'll bet my cottage on Gipsy Teapot to win," she declared and signed her bet. The big race was not the winning day for Gipsy Teapot who came in second. Lilac was told to be out of her home by Friday, three days' time.

As soon as Lilac got back to her cottage she went to the teapot to get the money to pay the bet but the teapot was empty – there was not a single penny in it. Lilac felt sick. "What am I going to do?" she asked herself. "I can't lose my home, I'll have to live like a tramp, what shall I do?" The only thing left in the pot was the piece of paper with the old lady's proverb written on it. Lilac read it again but still it did not make any sense to her.

As Lilac stood with the teapot in her hand she dropped it onto the floor and it smashed into a million pieces. Crying, she tried to put the pieces back together but the teapot was lost forever – it could never be mended. What was she going to do? She had no money, no teapot and no home. So Lilac started to drink. By the nighttime she was drunk and she had an idea. If she could get the betting note back she would be able to keep her cottage. Nobody knew of the bet except her and the bet man. Now, most nights he went to the tavern and got drunk before somehow walking home. "I'll wait for him and hit him with my stick, take my note and no-one will think it was me who hit him," she decided.

Late that night Lilac hid down the country lane that the betting man used to get home, and as he walked past her she hit him over the head with her walking stick, went through his pockets, found the bet and ran back to her cottage. Once there she burnt the note and then drank the night away.

They found Wilbert Snodling dead in Cowslip Lane. He had been hit with a large stick.

"Oh God, I have killed him!" Lilac cried. "But they don't know it's me, no-one can prove it was me!"

However, three days later, the soldiers came to her cottage asking to see her heavy walking stick and Lilac realised that she had left it in Cowslip Lane, next to the body. "I don't know where it is," she lied. "I haven't seen it since I moved into this cottage, why do you ask?"

"It was used to kill Wilbert Snodling in Cowslip Lane three days ago. Where were you?"

"I was here, I stayed in – I wasn't feeling well. I went to the tavern two days ago and I was told that he had been found dead. How do you know it was my stick?"

"You lent it to the tavern keeper when he fell down the stairs; as soon as he saw it he said it was yours. How can you lend someone a stick that you lost some time ago? The tavern keeper said he only gave it back to you a week ago. We hear you also lost your cottage over the County Grand Horse Race. You had a bet with Wilbert Snodling – he told many people about it."

"No, no! I did not kill him!"

"What was the name of the horse you bet on?"

"Gypsy Teapot. It came second."

"Didn't you hear?" the soldiers asked Lilac. "Gipsy Teapot was made the winner. Billy One was first but they found out that the owners had swapped him with a champion horse. You would have made a great deal of money and that would have made you a very rich woman but now we are taking you to prison on a murder charge for killing Wilbert Snodling with your walking stick on Cowslip Lane."

At the court Lilac was found guilty and sentenced to hang for murder. She was to be hanged at Hanging Tree Field two weeks later. The time came and as they put the rope around her neck all of her past came rushing back to her – her marriage, her son, the rabbits, the old lady in Little Bee Lane, the teapot, the horse and cart, her beautiful cottage and killing Wilbert Snodling. Moments before she fell through the trap door the words of the old lady's proverb came to her:

> What you are to the teapot
> So shall the teapot be to you
> Your heart will ache
> The pot will break
> For greediness you did make
> This tree will end thee

It was then the rabbit lady finally understood what it meant, but she knew no more because for her there was no more.

Two Sisters, One Secret

Nifan and Siena Backfield were both born in 1788 in a small village called Giggly Mount in Sumerset. In 1815 they were both working for Gabriel Farm, Nifan as a cowman and Siena a washerwoman and helper to the farmer's wife. Nifan and Siena married in 1820 and had their first baby, a little girl, who they called Lasan, and in 1822 their second baby, also a girl, called Tresha.

In the year 1824 life was hard but good and they were a close family. But in 1830 Nifan was killed in a bad storm – a tree branch snapped and fell on him. They didn't find his body until late afternoon the following day. Luckily for Siena the little old cottage was left to Nifan by his father so they still had a roof over their heads. Lasan was now eight years old and Tresha six. Siena told her children that she still had to work and that from now on they would have to look after each other. All was well until 1836 when old Farmer Gabriel sold his farm and the new farmer Eddoes laid off a lot of farm hands. Siena was one of them and now there was no money coming in.

Siena was a lovely girl to look at and she was also hard working but was known for her very bad temper. She was offered work in the local tavern where stagecoach travellers stayed the night. Siena's job was to take tankards of beer to the customers, bring back the empties and flirt to make the farmers, farm hands, highwaymen and robbers drink more ale. The job worked but Siena never saw her children – in the day she slept and at night she worked. Most times when she got back to the cottage she was drunk and had a man with her and slowly the two girls began to hate their mother – they never saw her and when they did she was drunk. They had to steal her money to buy food and second-hand clothes and shoes.

Siena would go around the cottage swearing and throwing things and the girls would hide until she left for the tavern. It was because of working in the tavern that she started to drink – ale, wine and anything that did not cost her money. Men paid her to sleep with them and with her bad temper many of the tavern girls got to know her vile mouth. To the tavern owner she could do no wrong. She knew this and played on it, it saved her job many times. One time the soldiers came to the tavern to arrest the owner for buying stolen wine and Siena slept with the captain and he dropped all the charges. From then on the Black Cock Tavern Inn was left alone and many stolen bottles of wine came in and went out again.

Linback Crow, the tavern owner, was soon a rich man and was starting to tire of Siena's drinking and fighting. Proper ladies were giving him attention – they were after his money but he didn't know this as he was too busy enjoying the attention. But he was a very tight man with his money and instead of keeping low about is dealings with stolen gear he started to brag. It wasn't long before the magistrates heard of this and sent the soldiers but the captain told Siena of the raid and so, once again, Siena saved Linback Crow from jail. He gave her money and she wanted to go to London to buy clothes but he said no and if she didn't like it she could leave the tavern. Now Siena hated him and told him he would pay but he laughed – how could she hurt him? She was just a tavern whore like all the rest that worked there.

All that night Siena drank ale and wine and all she could think about was that he had called her a tavern whore and she wanted him to pay for that. She had saved his neck and for what? To be called a common whore. Not once but twice she had saved him and now it was time for him to pay his debt.

She would wait and watch – she wondered where he hid his money.

She was lucky if she saw her children once a week and when they did see her they would run off and hide. It was nothing new – they had been doing it for years ever since their father was killed. The children stole money from her to buy food, clothes and shoes, even a new winter coat and between them they had stolen and hidden away nearly £300, but Siena had no idea about the stolen money.

It was December 1839 and only a week away from Christmas. Linback Crow had loads of stolen wine that he was selling stored in the stables at the back of the Tavern Inn. Siena knew this so she went to her lover, the captain, and told him. So with his troops he raided the Tavern Inn and found many bottles of wine. The captain informed Linback that if he paid him well he would leave, finding no wine. He wanted £500 and so Linback Crow paid him £500. When Siena and the captain were at their love nest, Siena asked for her £200 but the captain only gave her £50. She flew into a terrible rage, picked up a dagger and stabbed the captain to death, stole his £500 then ran off. No one saw her or knew that she was the captain's lover.

Her two daughters saw her coming down the lane and hid. They watched her move a big stone and hide the £500 in a bag under it. The daughters had found near the cottage a small stone house, which they had cleaned and made their home. They brought thick blankets, had lots of food, built up the fire and spent all day collecting wood – it was an ideal place for them to live and in the winter it was warm and dry. It had one small window and one very small strong door. That evening when their mother went to the Tavern Inn they lifted the stone and found bags of coins, over £500, that their mother had been stealing from Linback Crow.

It wasn't long before everyone heard about the murder of the captain but no one knew who did it. People started talking about the captain and his troopers going to the Tavern Inn to search for the stolen wine but they never found it, and then the next thing was that someone had murdered him. When the magistrate heard of this he called a lieutenant and told him he wanted him to raid the Black Cock Tavern Inn early in the morning, take 30 troopers and not to tell anyone, not even his troopers, for he was sure Linback Crow killed the captain to keep him quiet. "I have heard he has many barrels of French wine. When you find it, arrest Linback Crow and throw him in jail, then when he comes to my court I will have him hung. Now go and report to me in the morning."

Late that night the lieutenant raided the Black Cock Tavern Inn and found the barrels of French wine, arrested Linback Crow and threw him in jail. Siena knew nothing of this. The next day Linback stood in front of the magistrate. "Tell me who sold you the wine," he asked, "and I will not hang you this day."

"I will need some time, replied Linback.

"I will give you one week," replied the magistrate. Linback sent a message to Siena asking her to go and see him in jail. Siena went and Linback told her to go and see the O'Rialy gang and tell them to get him out of jail. He said to tell them he would give them £1,000.

"And what will you give me," asked Siena.

"More money than you have ever seen," replied Linback.

The next time Siena saw Linback she told him that the O'Rialy gang didn't trust him and they wanted the £1,000 first. "Tell me where your money is," asked Siena.

Although Linback didn't want to tell her, he didn't want to hang either. So he told her, "It's in the old dry well near the old oak tree."

Siena went to the old dry well and found many, many bags of coins – there must have been £20,000 in coins. Siena took all the bags back to her big stone and hid them there not knowing that her two daughters were watching her hide the money. Siena never went to the O'Rialy gang and a few days later as she watched Linback Crow hang, she thought to herself, "So I'm a common tavern whore but I'm alive and you will soon be dead. Soon I will leave here to go to London where I'll be a lady."

A few weeks later Siena got very drunk and got in a fight over a soldier with another young girl who she beat very badly. In a terrible rage she shouted at the girl that she was going to kill her. "I've killed once before, I've had a man hung and you will be number three," she screamed whilst kicking and hitting the girl who was lying on the floor. A man tried to drag her off but Siena grabbed a knife and stabbed him to death. The soldiers were called and she was taken to jail. The next day she stood in front of the magistrate who said she would hang for the murder. Siena shouted at the magistrate, swearing and spitting at him, but a few days later they hung her.

Siena's daughters knew of the murder and the hanging but kept away. Many of their friends wanted to take them both in but they refused and they moved back into the cottage. Now young ladies, Lasan and Tresha sat talking. "Let's stay here for a year," said Lasan, "then we can leave. We can say we are going to stay with our father's brother." So they kept themselves to themselves and when the year was up they told their friends they were going to visit their uncle in Reading. They left, taking just a travel bag each, which they had packed with all the hidden money. They took a coach to Reading in Berkshire and then another coach to London where they got a room in a small hotel.

The next day they found a bank and deposited all the money and were surprised to find it amounted to £35,433. They told the bank manager that it was money left to them by their mother after she died. They split the money between them and changed their names to Pettet and Rassea Halldan from Brighton. They stayed at the hotel for six months, reading all the newspapers, but nothing was reported about them.

One night a young doctor came to stay at the hotel and on meeting Pettet and her sister immediately fell in love with Pettet and by the end of the evening all three were friends. After a year the doctor asked Pettet out and two months later they were married. Rassea met a solicitor at a party and six months after Pettet married, Rassea married her solicitor and the four of them moved from London to Bury St Edmunds. Pettet helped her husband set up his doctor's practice and bought a house not far away from her sister Rassea, who was also helping her husband to build up his solicitor's practice. Pettet had three children – two girls and a boy – and lived very happily until she died in 1900 aged 80 years old. Her sister Rassea died in 1902 also at the age of 80 and both took their secret to the grave. They never told their husbands of their past and when they died the past died with them.

Somewhere out there today are the great, great, grandchildren of Pettet and Rassea and they will never know that their great grandmother has hung for murder.

The Willow

Long Tree Way is a long and narrow road; they say that in the 18th century it was a country road that led to a big manor house but today the house has gone and instead there is a big factory estate. Long Tree Way is now a long road with small terraced houses on both sides that was developed in the 1920s; at number 127 lives Roger Jones.

Roger is 30 years old, single and lives alone. Roger was born in the house where he lived with his mother and father up until seven years ago when his father died leaving just Roger and his mother. Then two years ago she passed away leaving the house to Roger. Roger works as a civil servant in a nine to four-thirty job, which he tells everyone is boring but is, in fact, far from it because Roger works at MI 11. MI 11 got its name because there are 11 people in the department – Roger, his boss Colonel Lenten Lee Brewer, Major Herman, Cane Lilac Sanderson and seven other agents. MI 11 is an assassination organisation that takes out any foreign agents who could be a danger to England. No one outside MI 11 knows of Roger's work.

At the time of this story there was an enquiry going on inside MI 11. Someone had leaked information that two agents had been killed and one badly injured and the colonel had asked Roger Jones to find out who it was.

Roger told everyone within the department that his mother always called him Jona and so this is the name he was known by. The colonel had told Jona that a Mr Hezentash would call at his house at eight o'clock that night with information on the leak inside MI 11 and almost directly on the hour the doorbell at number 127 rang.

Standing on Jona's doorstep was a small, thin man with receding hair who was about 50 years old. "Good evening, Mr Jones," said the man, "my name is Mr Hezentash, you were expecting me?" Mr Hezentash was an agent from the Mexican government.

"Yes, yes come in," said Jona.

On entering the house the stranger said, "Let us go into your garden for walls have ears. Let us walk while we talk."

From his pocket Mr Hezentash took out a small black box, switched it on and turned around in the garden with the box in front of him. "This box will tell me if your home or garden is bugged," he explained to Roger. The garden was bugged – Roger had two garden gnomes and one had a small chip that could record everything whilst the other hid an aerial to pick up the sound. These were placed in order to record everything Mr Hezentash said. The box in his hand could block the chip and stop anything being recorded but Jona had a special MI 11 ring, which could reverse the block and so without the stranger being aware he would in fact be clearly recorded.

"Mr Jones, I can only stay for 15 minutes and then I must leave. Agent Bradfield is passing on information to General Benzoin Zacapokra who is leaving the country for Russia on Friday. He is staying at the Belling Hotel in Paddington. Mr Jones, he must not leave with the information he has been given. The general is in room 316a on the third floor – there are two guards outside his room and one guard stationed in the lobby, they change over every three hours. You have three hours to get in and out at some point within the next 24 hours – you can choose your own time. If this information gets out many agents will suffer – all over the world. Need I say more?"

"No, who else knows where General Zacapokra is?" asked Jona.

"Bradfield, you, myself and one other who works for him," replied Mr Hezentash. Then, looking at his watch, Mr Hezentash said he must go and the men shook hands. Jona decided that he would, that very night, take out General Zacapokra. He put a few things together, made a few phone calls and by 9pm he was ready to go.

At 9.58pm Roger Jones walked into the lobby of the Belling Hotel and took the lift to the second floor. From there he used the stairs to the third level and noticed two men sitting outside the general's room. He watched them for some time and concluded something was not quite right – they sat but did not move. Jona walked towards the guards and they did not look up or stand up or notice him at all. When Jona got closer to them he realised that they were both drugged or dead, and upon checking them he discovered they were in fact dead. Drawing his gun, Jona tried the door of the room – it opened to reveal the general with a hole through his head lying dead on the bed – he had been killed with a PRK silencer. Quickly going through the room and the general's belongings, he found a small chip hidden behind the badge of his uniform cap. Jona took it out and quickly left the hotel.

Who had killed the general? Who had killed his bodyguards? Roger knew he could not go home with the chip straight away in case he had been seen, so he drove around for half an hour to make sure that he was not being followed then he went to a secret location. Jona parked his car in a hotel, booked a room and went into the bar to have a drink. He sat where he could see the doors to the lobby and waited.

At precisely 11.30 two men entered the hotel and caught sight of Jona. They ordered drinks and sat down a few tables away by the bar wall. People started to drift into the bar and Jona thought this would be a good time to see if they were following him. He stood up and walked into the hotel clothes shop and stood in front of the shop mirror where he could see the bar doors. After a short time the two men walked out looking from left to right. One man walked off to the right and the other one went left. Jona went back into the bar, made a call, and sat back down.

Five minutes later the police arrived and, on seeing the two men, they walked over and started to talk to them. Jona took this opportunity to slip out of the hotel and walk back to his flat. When Jona arrived he phoned the hotel and asked to speak to the police and informed them that the two men they were speaking to were not the men they were looking for and to let them go.

The hotel detective was told to go and pick up the glasses that the two men had been drinking out of so that they could be checked for fingerprints. At 12.30 Jona got a call informing him of the names of the two men and telling him that they were bodyguards for General Benzoin Zacapokra. Jona hid the chip in a place where it would never be found, had something to eat and went to bed.

At the offices of MI 11 he told his boss exactly what had happened but didn't tell him that he had found the chip. His boss asked him if he had found any papers and Jona informed him that the only papers he found were about the general and that he didn't think he had the chip as nothing in the room had been touched. He informed him that he thought it was a hit and run, taking out the bodyguards in order to be able to get to the general. "Who do you think it could be?" asked Jona.

"It could be his own people. There have been a lot of stories about him – missing money, drugs…One of their top agents was found dead, only the general knew who and where he was," replied his boss. Looking at Jona his boss said that he had done a good job so far but he needed to find that chip. Smiling, he told Jona, "Get out of here, I've got work to do."

Jona went to his office and found Bradfield there. "I've been looking for you, they told me you were in," said Bradfield.

"What can I do for you?" asked Jona.

"I hear that the general was found dead in his hotel room. The old man just told me. He was the last person I would have thought would be killed. I didn't know he was over here, did you?" asked Bradfield.

"No," replied Jona, "why was he over here?"

"I don't know," said Bradfield, "do you?"

"No," said Jona, "but the old man wants me to find out more."

Jona asked Bradfield what he was up to and Bradfield informed him that he was taking a few days' holiday. "I'm going over to see my old friend Ken Taylor in New York," Bradfield said. "He will be 70 next Sunday; he doesn't know I'm going so it will be a big surprise."

"If I don't see you before you go, have a good trip," said Jona.

"Thanks," said Bradfield as he left Jona's office.

As Jona sat at his desk he noticed that someone had tried to open his drawer. Laughing to himself, he thought, "Won't they ever learn?"

It was Tuesday and he would be flying out on Friday but before then he had work to do. The next day, Wednesday, he got a phone call from Lilac Sanderson, the secretary, informing him that Mr Hezentash had been killed by a hit-and-run driver. They didn't know who had killed him or even who wanted him dead, and told him not to speak to anyone about Mr Hezentash. Jona wondered, if Lilac Sanderson knew about Hezentash, just how many other people knew about him? Did they know of Hezentash's visit to Jona? Was he the next on the list? Jona decided that whoever was involved wanted him alive to lead them to the chip and then it would be 'goodnight Mr Jones'.

At home, whilst looking for some keys, Jona found three notes his mother had left a long time ago. One was the last one she gave him and it took his mind back to the day he had visited the family solicitors, Wilson, Wilson and Burn. His mother had died ten days previously and the visit was for the reading of her will.

To my son, Roger

I leave my house in Long Tree Way, £20,000 I have in my bank account which your father left with me together with many shares that I have never touched.

Mr Wilson will help you find out more about your father's shares.

Your loving mother
Mrs Rose Jones

Mr Wilson informed Roger that he had a letter for him from his mother, which had been left with them to be given to Roger on her death. He gave Roger the letter and said if there was anything in the letter he could help him with, to give him a call.

When Roger returned home he opened his mother's letter and it started like this:

Dear Son

Over the years we have had lots of fun but this is my last note to you. I played this game many times with your father, right up to the day he died. I'd give lots of clues for him to find and at the end of each clue there was a number of Xs. One X meaning something to do with clothes, two Xs food, three Xs person or persons, four Xs not good. Now the idea of the game is that I would give him a clue, such as telling him where I had put his birthday present. The clues would tell him where and he would remember the clues for the rest of his life. He also played games on me and it was our secret, which we never told anyone. I'll show you how the game worked...

Son
In Frame Road there are two
That's your first clue

In his song it cried for him
Starts with school, second clue

He ran and ran to catch his van
Your bike was old and rusty
Being left in a field and park
Third clue

You once slipped and hurt your back
Your little friend Jack brought you home
Clue not been stalk, fourth clue

Don't sit upon your seat there's new faces you must meet.

Son, forgive those you love – Mr Wilson has. One more letter to give you but only when you have read this letter. You must say that you know TJ one, TJ two. You must tell him what the two TJs stand for. If you can't do this, Mr Wilson will not give you my letter. If what you say is correct, then Mr Wilson will open the letter and give it to you.

Forgive but not forget,
Mum
XXX

Anyone else reading this note would not have a clue what it means but over the years both could pick up clues from each other's notes. They called this game 'Give Us A Clue'. Roger sat down and started to break down his mother's last clue note.

In Frame Road the last two houses had the same number, 146. The last but one house was owned by Mr and Mrs Reading and the last house was owned by Mr and Mrs Reading's daughter and her husband. They had made a door between the two houses so that they could easily go from one house to the other without going outside.

In the next clue *Willow Weep For Me* sung by Sam Cook, starting with school, the first two letters are SC (Sam Cook). So we now have 146 The Willow.

The next clue 'He ran and ran to catch his van' – David Bedford, Bedford Road. The bike was left in Ruston Park. So now it reads, 146 The Willow, Bedford Road, Ruston Park.

The last clue, the name of the boy who bought him home was called Tom not Jack – the last part was telling him to go to this address and ask for Tom.

As soon as possible, once he had been to this address, he would know what TJ one and TJ two stood for.

It took Jona some time to work it out but as he had played this game for so many hours he got to know his mother's way of playing the game – by giving him clues on the things she knew he knew. The next day he went to 146 The Willow, Bedford Road, Ruston Park and knocked on the door and waited. After some time, as he was just about to knock again, the door was opened by a young woman in her late 20s holding a baby. As soon as she saw him she put her hand to her mouth and said, "Oh my God!" and just stood and stared at Roger.

"I'm sorry to bother you but does Tom live here?" he asked.

"Yes," said the young woman.

"Is he in?" asked Roger.

"Yes," she replied.

"Would it be possible for me to have a word with him?" asked Roger.

"Yes, please do come in – Tom is in the garden." She called out to Tom and he came in from the garden. On seeing Roger he stopped and stared.

Roger stared back at Tom – they were struck by the fact that they were identical!

Tom's wife said, "I can't believe it! He's your double."

"Who are you?" asked Tom.

"My name is Roger Jones and I live in Middleton,"

"My name is Tom Jones," Tom replied.

Roger looked down at the baby and asked Tom if he was his son. "Don't tell me his name," said Roger. Taking out a piece of paper with the game written on, he read the last part:

The Lord's Prayer will tell you, the lights are green
Brighter than you've ever seen
Now go to Mr Wilson and answer his question.
Mrs Shoe will tell you who's mum is the name of your son called Tom after you
Yes, The Lords Prayer
Read to Roger in the name of the father and the son.

Tom said "Who are you? And why have you come here to our house? What do you want – money?"

"No, no, no, I was given your address. My mother told me to call," said Roger

"Why would she do that?" asked Tom,

"I don't know," said Roger.

"What do you mean, you don't know?" said Tom.

Roger explained that his mother had died two weeks ago and that he had been given the letter at the reading of his mother's will by the family solicitors. "The letter asked me to solve some clues so that I can answer a question the solicitor had for me. If I answered correctly, he would give me a letter telling me everything. That's why I'm here," said Roger. "Maybe we could talk, we might be able to find out what this means."

Tom thought this was a good idea and told Roger to ask any questions he wanted. Roger asked Tom if his son's name was Tom Jones.

"Yes," said Tom

He then asked Tom if his mother and father were still alive.

"No," said Tom, "they both died in a car crash six years ago."

Roger asked Tom if he had any brothers or sisters, and Tom told him that he didn't, at least not that he knew of. Roger went on to ask if Tom had any living relatives on his mother or father's side and again Tom told Roger that as far as he knew there were none.

"So," said Roger, "it's possible you could be an only child.

"Yes," said Tom.

Roger looked at Tom and said that everything he had said was the same for him. "I have no mother, no father or brothers and sisters and we have the same name – Jones." Then Roger asked Tom how old he was.

"I'm 30, I was born on 24th July 1977."

"That's the same birthday as mine," said Roger, "we are like two peas in a pod, we could be twins. We have the same voice, the same build, we're roughly the same weight and have the same hair colour."

Tom looked at Roger. "I don't know what to say," he said, and so for the next three hours they talked. Eventually Roger told Tom that he would come back in a couple of days once he had got the letter from his solicitor. Roger asked Tom what he did for a living and Tom told him that he owned two paint shops. "We make a very good living." And he asked Roger what he did.

"I'm a civil servant, checking out people and finding people the service want to talk to," he replied. "It's a good job but I'm only there for the money and perks.

Tom's wife's name was Jill and whilst this was all going on she couldn't stop staring at Roger, never once taking her eyes off him.

That night Roger found it really hard to sleep as his head was in such a spin. The next morning he went to see his solicitor. Mr Wilson told Roger that he had two letters for him but that he would have to answer a question. He opened the first letter and read out the Lord's Prayer. "What's your answer, Mr Jones?"

"Like father like son, in the prayer it reads 'in the name of the father and the son'," said Roger.

"Yes, that's what your mother has written," replied Mr Wilson. "I can now give you your mother's last letter. Please let me know if I can be of any help to you in the future."

With that Roger shook hands with Mr Wilson and left. When Roger got home, he opened the letter and she had started her letter exactly the same way as she always started her notes…

Dear Son

I know you would solve my last clue game before you read this letter. Please don't judge me badly but at the time it was out of my hands. Until my dying date I would say it was the best thing your father and I could do and over the years it has proved to me that your father and I were right.

When you were born on 24th July 1977 at Middleton General Hospital, I didn't just give birth to you, I gave birth to twins. I was very ill after the birth and nearly died. I spent a very long time in hospital whilst your father took you both home. You were both in fine health but to help your father look after you, your father's brother and his wife came to stay. A few months earlier his brother and his wife had lost their baby – he was only two weeks old, and she was told that she couldn't have any more children. A very dear friend of mine, Mrs Shoe, offered to help to bring you up knowing that your father felt it would be too much for us, what with me in hospital and him still having to go to work. But your father thought it would be best to ask his brother and his wife to look after one of you and they jumped at the chance. They said they would take your brother and, as you know, they called him Tom. When I came home from hospital and I saw how much they loved your brother, I couldn't take him back. I also knew that I wouldn't be able to bring up the two of you; even though I was at home there was still a lot of things I couldn't do.

So with great pain we told them that they could keep your brother but decided that you should never be told what we had done. It was also decided that I would be the only one who knew where they lived so that I could still see your brother as he grew up, and for the last 30 years that is what I have done. Many times I have wanted to tell you and have spent many nights crying for having given your brother away. Slowly I got better and then sadly your father died. We gave your uncle Tom's birth certificate and as he had the same name we somehow got away with it and everyone accepted that Tom was their son.

It didn't matter that there was no adoption – the most important thing was that they gave your brother a very happy life and he loved them very much. They were a very happy family. Then, as you know by now, they both died in a car crash. It took Tom a very long time to get over their death and it caused me a lot of pain as I could not go to him because he didn't know who I was. But God was looking down on your brother as about two months after their death he met his wife Jill. She pulled him back together and now, as you saw for yourself, he is a very happy man.

Your father and I decided not to tell you that your father had a brother. We didn't want to lie to you by saying he was dead, moved abroad or that they fell out or that we just didn't know where he was, just in case you decided to look for him. All I ask of you, Son, is not to be angry with me and to forgive me and your father for what we did.

Reading his mother's letter brought tears to his eyes. Oh how he loved his mother – all those years carrying such a secret. The pain she must have gone through giving away her son and not being able to tell her other son that he had a brother living less than 40 miles away. He looked at their photo and said that there was nothing to forgive. "I love you Mum and Dad, you are the bravest people I will ever know, I'm so proud of you both. I promise Tom will know everything and, like me, be very proud of you both.

The letter finished off with one last clue:

The Shoe has a tongue that can speak.

Live a good life, Son, find a wife and give us a grandson. But most of all, when things are not going too well, talk to us and we will help you. Your father wasn't a man to say I love you but he loved you very much. I knew he loved us both very much and when he died I missed him so very much but now we are together again forever. Make up for the years you have lost with your brother, for now you have a family.

Goodbye my son
Mum
XXX

That evening he rang Tom and asked if he could go and see them both. He told them he had a letter he would like them both to read. So the next afternoon Roger went to see Tom and Jill. After talking to them both for a while, Roger gave them the letter and before they read it Roger asked them to please not think too badly of her. Tom and Jill sat and read the letter together and as they read Roger sat and watched them as tears started to fall down both their cheeks. Tom put the letter down and said to Roger, "Come here, brother," and they hugged and cried for a long time, three people crying with joy, sadness, love and memories, but most of all with the joy of finding one and other.

They invited Roger to stay the night and as he'd promised, he told them all about their mum and dad, even the next day they all found it hard not to cry. Tom read his mother's letter over and over. Roger loved his brother and his new nephew. It sounded silly – he had lost his family and found his family and he felt so happy and proud.

Roger asked Tom if the name Shoe meant anything to him. Tom said that his mum had an old friend call Mrs Shoe, they had been friends of the family for as long as he could remember. "Why do you ask?" said Tom.

"Because Mum wants us to talk to her about us," said Roger.

"I wonder what 'a shoe that can speak' means," said Tom. "I'll give her a call and ask her to come over." Tom phoned Mrs Shoe and arranged for a taxi to pick her up and bring her over to Tom's house. Whilst she was on her way, Tom and Roger decided to have some fun – they decided that Roger would answer the door and tell her to go into the lounge, then Roger would stay back whilst Tom walked into the lounge. As they were dressed very differently, she would almost certainly question him on the fact that he was wearing jeans when he answered the door and at that point Roger would walk in. So they did just that and poor Mrs Shoe did exactly what they said she would do – stared and Roger and Tom and then burst into tears. When they told her about the letter she told them how she had looked after the two of them when their mother was in hospital, how ill she was and how their father's brother and his wife took Tom and brought him up as their own. And that all through the years they kept their mother informed of how Tom was doing. Everything she told them was in the letter and later, when she had finished her story, they gave her the letter to read. Mrs Shoe told Roger lots more that he didn't know. She said, "I've kept this secret for 30 years. I've watched and felt the pain your mother suffered and your father was never the same once Tom had been taken away. He once told me that he found it hard to tell Roger that he loved him. All that your mother and father did was for the love of you both. You must always remember that sometimes you have to do things that break your heart because you know it's the right thing to do. I'm proud to say they did the right thing – you have a lifetime to make up and get to know each other."

Putting down the note, Jona smiled. And as he thought about that letter – he had been given it over two years ago – a lot had passed since then. Tom and Jill had another baby, this time a girl, and they had called her Jill.

*

Jona's phone rang – it was his boss. He asked Jona to come to the office as he needed to talk to him. When Jona arrived his boss asked him if he knew General Benzoin Zacapokra was a top spy for Parraz Agency.

"Yes," said Jona.

"You did?" asked his boss.

"Yes," said Jona, "isn't that what you pay me to know?"

"Do you know who killed him?" asked his boss.

"I don't know," said Jona, "but whoever it was saved us the job."

"What are you going to do next?…No don't tell me," said his boss.

Jona had no intention of telling him anything. He was going to his old friend Martin Artman, so that he could help him read the chip. Jona arranged to meet Martin in the park where he told him about the general and the chip and Martin told Jona to bring the chip to his house that night. When Roger read the chip his blood ran cold. There were 80 names of agents from all over the world – codes, dates and places. If the general had left the country with this information there could have been a world war three. It also told him the name of the man at the top of Parraz Agency. He could not believe that it was the name of a lifelong friend. He didn't have to look at the address, he knew it off by heart, and he knew he would have to take him out as soon as possible.

Jona knew that he was being followed 24 hours a day and that they were too good at their job to shake them off. He asked Martin if he could help him get a passport urgently as he had to leave the country but that he would be back in five days. Martin told Jona that he could help but it would cost £500 and take two days to arrange. Jona arranged to meet with Martin in two days' time.

When Jona got home he phoned Tom, using a mobile Martin had given him. Over the past two years Roger and Tom had become very close, and he asked if he could meet him for a pint; he told him that it was important. Tom asked him what it was all about but Roger told him not to ask any questions and he would tell him when they met. They arranged to meet at the Red Lion in Cap Field at seven o'clock. Roger asked Tom not to say anything to Jill or anyone else about where they were going as it was important that no one knew.

Before his meeting with Tom, Jona had to see Martin. Martin was waiting for him and told Jona that when he left he wouldn't recognise himself and Martin was right. Jona walked right past the four agents that had been following him and were waiting for him outside, he walked up to a parked car, got in and drove away. At the Red Lion he saw Tom sitting on his own. He walked up to him and sat down at a table beside him. Roger sat there until eight o'clock making sure that no one was taking any notice of them. The bar was half full but there was no one sitting near them. When Roger was sure he hadn't been followed he said hello to Tom. "Roger," said Tom, recognising his voice.

"Yes," said Roger. "Just listen…I need you to take my place for the next five days. I have to go away but it's important that people think I am in Middleton. I'm being followed and I need your help. I can't say too much, only that when it's over many people will have died. I will tell you everything when it's over but for now all you have to do is stay at my house and drive around in my car. I need these people to see you. They won't harm you, they will just follow you wherever you go. Don't phone Jill or your work from my house as the phone is bugged. Use my private mobile for any calls you want to make but don't use it in the house or the car as they are also bugged. I don't like asking you, Tom, but you are the only person who can do this for me.

"I'll do whatever I can," said Tom, "but please tell me what's going on."

"I can only tell you that you need to carry my old mobile with you at all times. Do not use it and do not answer it if it rings," said Roger. "It's very important that you remember this." The spare keys to my house are under the flowerpot to the left of the front door. We will meet one more time and I will give you the car keys and door keys and tell you more. I'll ring you on your mobile. I'll be leaving soon but please do not leave for another hour." He asked Tom if he could meet him in the Lady Grey pub in Linton in two days' time at seven o'clock. Tom agreed and with that Roger got up and left.

Martin had the passport, clothing and tickets to New York all packed in a holdall ready for Jona when he arrived. Jona would be flying out from Heathrow on the next Monday and Martin had arranged for a car to pick him up and bring him back from the airport, however the ticket to New York was only one-way. Jona would be flying back from San Francisco. He would be staying at the Golden Bridge Hotel for one night where a room had been booked for him in the name of Davis Foreland. Someone would meet him there with his ticket, a new passport and some money. The hotel bill had been paid in advance so he would stay in his room, only going to the hotel restaurant for his meal.

When Roger walked into the Lady Grey pub, Tom was waiting. They did the same as before and when Roger was sure he hadn't been followed he spoke to Tom. "Listen well, Tom. Leave your house and catch a train. Be at the Ockbarn Café at seven o'clock – that's where I go for my breakfast. You must be there by seven o'clock every morning for you will be watched. Leave whenever you're ready and buy a paper from the shop next door – the Daily Mail – then walk slowly back to my house. I want them to see you and follow you. Stay in the house but remember don't make any phone calls, then after a while go for a walk then go back to the house and stay in – don't go out again. Leave the lights and TV on. Make sure you let them know you are in the house. The next day go to the café and then go for a bus ride. Do anything you want but don't get in touch with any friends, be very careful. Here are the car keys and the door keys and my house phone number. Remember it. Most of all, let them see you as much as you can – it's important they don't panic by losing sight of you. I will be back within five days. Here's £500 to buy shirts and trousers… whatever you want. I've told my boss to let it be known that I am on holiday for a week. If anything goes wrong with the mobile ring 7777 555 433 and say 'red switch off' – they will do the rest. The people that are following you are also being followed, like cat and mouse.

For a hour Roger told Tom a few things and answered many of his questions and told him that when he heard "A hundred pounds for a shirt, you must be joking," then he would know Roger was back. I thank you, Tom, and England thanks you." Tom wished Roger good luck and with that, Roger quickly left the Lady Grey pub. An hour later Tom got up and left with the words rushing through his brain "England thanks you".

Everything went to plan. Jona flew out to New York and went to the hotel that had been booked for him for one night. The next day he took a train to Buffalo. He walked to a nearby apartment, one he knew very well, watching until he saw who he was waiting for. He knew the man's routine inside and out and at seven o'clock that night he knocked on his door – 164 Rudde de Mont. When he door opened the man said, "Roger, come in, come in." At 7.05pm Roger left the apartment leaving one dead body lying on a bed with a broken neck, and took a train back to New York City.

Roger went back to his hotel staying in his room all night and booked out the next morning, telling reception that his next meeting was in Miami. He took a train to San Francisco and booked into the Golden Bridge Hotel as arranged, picked up his documents and flew back to Heathrow the next day, where he was picked up by car and taken to a safe house. He burnt his fake passports, tickets and clothing, put on his own clothes and was ready to take his place again.

Tom was sitting in the café having his breakfast as two men passed his table. He heard one of them say, "A hundred pounds for a shirt, you must to be joking," and he knew that Roger was back.

The next day when he went to the café the lady owner, mistaking him for Roger, asked him if he could help lift a box for her. "It's in the kitchen," she said.

"Of course," said Tom and followed her to the kitchen where a man was waiting. He told Tom to follow him and told Tom to get into a van that was outside waiting for them. As it drove away the lady walked back into the café and thanked Roger for his help. Roger was back and Tom was on his way home.

Outside the café four men watched as Roger came out, bought his Daily Mail and walked back to his house, mission complete. As he was walking home he thought, "Now, Mr Big, it's your turn – or should he say 'Miss Big'." He went out for a meal and rang Tom to thank him for all he had done.

"No trouble, I loved it," said Tom.

"Good," said Roger, "I'll see you all very soon, don't get in touch."

On Monday he was back in his office. His boss rang and told him to go up and see him. "Let's go for a walk," his boss said. "I want them to see us together, what have you got for me?"

Jona told him that Mr Big was in MI 11.

"Are you sure," asked his boss, "Who is it? Is it Lilac Sanderson, my secretary?"

"Yes," said Jona, "it's a hundred percent. She must be taken out right away, tonight."

"It will be done," said his boss.

Jona told him that he would give him the chip tomorrow and that it told them everything they needed to know. The general and Lilac were lovers who met a long time ago when they both worked for Parraz. The general cost the lives of four of their agents and they were going to kill him but Lilac begged for his life and they made her a deal. They would let him live if she went to England and worked for the MI 11. How they got her in, he didn't know, but they did and knowing how clever she was, it didn't take long before she had worked her way up to becoming his secretary. There was also someone high up helping her and she had no one looking over her shoulder so she was able to log into every country – getting names, addresses and any information they wanted, logging everything onto the chip. The general came over to take the chip back, but he was going to sell it to the Russians, Parraz found out and killed him. Lilac had arranged to go with the general and when they killed him they didn't know that he had the chip on him. The chip showed the code for Parraz was "It's hot today, I'll change my shoes" and Jona told his boss, who had heard Lilac say this a lot of times when she was on the phone.

"So," said his boss, "she is the one we have been looking for, she has been giving out information about our agents – names, addresses, places and everything has been put onto this chip. But that means we still don't know who number one is."

"Their number one is dead," said Jona "It's Ken Taylor, her father."

"Her father," replied his boss. "So that's how she got in."

"He told people that he didn't want anyone to know she was his daughter and when he retired he went over to them," said, Jona, "And anything he wanted to know, she told him."

"He was your friend," said his boss.

"Yes," said Jona, "a very close friend and when he left MI 11 he became the top man for Parraz."

"How do you know he's dead?" asked his boss.

"I've only just found out myself. They found him in his apartment with his neck broken. If we hadn't been following the people following you all week, I would have said you killed him, but I know you didn't."

Jona could account for every day he was out of the country as he had asked Tom to write down everything he did every day so that he could answer any questions asked by his boss.

"So let's get it straight," said his boss. "You're saying the general came over to pick up the chip, that Ken Taylor's daughter gave it to him and he was going to take it to America to give to Ken Taylor. But instead he was going to take it to Russia to sell to the Russians and Lilac Sanderson was going with him. He got the chip but before he could leave the country he and his two bodyguards were killed. You found the chip and you found out what was on it. The general must have known his killer to let him into his hotel room. You hid the chip, someone killed Ken Taylor in New York – that someone not being you because you were being watched 24 hours a day. Someone killed Hezentash in a hit-and-run who we have yet to find. How am I doing so far? Now, as you say,we have to take out Lilac in the next 12 hours and the chip has to be destroyed so that no one else can get hold of it."

As his boss was talking, warning bells started ringing – how did he know what was on the chip? He'd never told him. Was he in with Lilac? Did he have Hezentash killed after he put Hezentash on to him and the general to take away anything to do with him. Clever.

After leaving his boss he rang a man called George. They met two hours later and he told George everything. The next day his boss, Lenton Lee Brewer, was found dead in his car – he had been shot. Lilac Sanderson was also found dead – her body was found floating in the river. Jona gave George the chip but not before he had a copy made. Were his boss and Lilac lovers, or did she double-cross him, or did he double cross her? That Jona would never know. Lilac made the mistake of going to the general and whatever happened there were now seven dead, but thankfully the chip was in safe hands. Jona was told that he would be getting a new boss, Mr Porridge. He thought he had better take him some milk in as there would almost certainly be a few jokes about his name.

Laughing to himself, he rang Tom, his big brother. For Mrs Shoe told them Tom was born first by nearly two minutes. He told Tom that he would be over in about two hours as he had a few things to tidy up first. "Are you ok, Roger?" asked Tom.

"Yes," said Roger, "I'm looking forward to catching up with you."

On his way over to Tom and Jill's he went over a few things – Bradfield was the giveaway, putting him on the wrong trail, killing Hezentash again, pointing him in the wrong direction, the general's death, along with his two bodyguards. But they made one mistake in taking him for a fool. That he most definitely was not. That's why there were seven people dead and he had the chip and was alive and on his way to see his family.

The Pretender

The McCoil family lived on the banks of the Mississippi River, in a place called Cotton Tower. It was called Cotton Tower because the McCoils owned four cotton plantations spread along the Mississippi and lived in a house that was shaped like a tower. On 17th May 1701 Major Cane McCoil received a letter he had been waiting for, for many months. "At last!" he cried to his wife.

"Read it, read it!" she said.

After reading the letter again and again, he looked at his wife and said, "She will be here in ten days' time. Now I need to find a captain for her – the best there is and the best captain around, if you can find him, is Red Burlington. The last I heard he was in St Louis. I'll send someone to find him and bring him by telling him that I've got a ship for him but we'll have to make sure this is done within the week."

Red Burlington arrived at Cotton Tower six days later. He was 30 years old, was born in St Louis and lived and worked on the Mississippi all his life. He stood 6ft 6in and weighed about 20 stone, a powerful man who, as a boy, had bright red hair – and that was the reason he was called Red. He started working on the river from the age of ten and had done just about every job there was. He knew every bend, twist, creek, currents and shallow or deep water. He had been a captain's boy, galley boy, deck boy, wood boy loading hand, bosun's mate, second mate and was now a captain, which he'd achieved by working hard. He never married – his first love had died in his arms and he said that he would never find anyone to take her place. After this he took to fighting and, being a big man, won more fights than he lost. He had a good name on the river as a captain and he was proud of it. He knew everything there was to know about the boats that went up and down the river from the row boards to the paddle steamers, and now he was being asked to be the captain of a sailing ship called *The Pretender,* which was 80ft long, 60 tonnes, with a 15-man crew. If he was ever asked why he had such a big crew his answer would always be "that's my business" and that's all you ever got from him.

Major McCoil was only 5ft 4in tall and slim built, his wife 5ft tall and very petite. She was loved by everyone and they always had friends calling both day and night. Beth and Cain McCoil had four children – three girls and one boy – and they were a very close family. The eldest girl was called Beth after her mother, the second daughter was called Kerry after her mother's mother and the third was called Grace, just because they liked the name. The boy was called Morgan after his father's father. Major McCoil had been a cavalry officer in the Union Army but had left the army on medical grounds. He then went to work for his father on his cotton plantation, which he inherited on his father's death. He worked hard on the plantation and over time built another three more, making him a very rich and powerful man on the river.

When Major McCoil saw Red Burlington walking up to his house he called his wife to come quick. They welcomed him and showed him into the study where a Mr and Mrs Stern Brace were talking to the plantation overseer. They turned as Red Burlington walked into the room, looking up to him as he was looking down. "Ah, Captain Burlington! Welcome…what would you like to drink?"

"Nothing, thank you, sir," replied Red. "I'm here on business, maybe afterwards?"

Just then Beth and the Major walked in. "Captain Burlington, have you met my friends?" asked Cane.

"Yes," he replied and the Major asked everyone to sit down. They sat and talked for the next four hours until they were told that dinner was ready to be served. "You must stay overnight," said the Major, "as I want to show you around the plantations."

So with a full belly and plenty of wine the captain was more than happy to stay.

Later that evening Major McCoil was sent news that *The Pretender* was at anchor at the mouth of the Mississippi. He sent for Red Burlington and told him but Red had already heard the news, to the Major's surprise.

"I'm not a river captain for nothing," he said.

Impressed, the Major said, "Well done, Captain, do you think you can be under sail in 15 days?"

"If you do your part," the replied Red Burlington, "I can be under sail in ten days."

"Great," said the Major. "I can see that you and I will get on well. Have you got your crew?"

"Yes," said Red, "they are ready and waiting."

The Major informed Red that his cargo would be on its way down river the next day and that his wife and friends wanted to go aboard *The Pretender*, and would be there on the next Sunday.

That Sunday the captain arrived with his crew on a steamer and could see the Major and Mrs McCoil and their friends heading for the ship in a longboat. But as if death were waiting on board, as soon as Major McCoil put one foot on the deck, he dropped down dead – they said it was a heart attack. A few days later Mrs McCoil came aboard and informed the captain that from this day *The Pretender* would sail flying a black flag that must never be taken down. The black flag would remain for as long as *The Pretender* sailed under the name of McCoil. "Do you understand, Captain," she asked.

"Yes Ma'am," he said.

"And as Major McCoil died at six o'clock, you will ring ship's bell at this time and all the crew must tip their hat or cap," she instructed.

"It will be done as you have asked, Mrs McCoil. As captain I will see to it," he replied.

That was the last time Red Burlington saw Mrs McCoil, for four weeks later she too dropped dead.

The captain and his crew worked night and day loading the cargo, cotton, deer hides, buffalo hides and indigo, together with enough fresh water, fruit and meat. Captain Burlington had said they would be away for anything up to four months so they needed enough provisions for this time away at sea. The captain was asked by a Mr Tregal if he had any room for more cargo as he had some coffee crates, timber and some more skins he needed to be shipped. The captain told him to bring them and he would find room. Only the captain and Mr Tregal knew what was actually in the crates – there were six of them and they were very heavy. He instructed his crew to put three crates on each side of the ship, and so it was done.

One of the crew was called 'Old Joe One Hand'. He had always sailed with Burlington and he would say that someone had to look after him, but he loved Burlington like a son. Joe had lost his hand swimming in the Mississippi river after being attacked by a crocodile. There were many ways to be killed on the river – crocodiles, cold, fast currents and Indians; the river was no place for weak men or men that couldn't swim. There were many tribes of Indians living along the riverbank – Biloxia, Bayogoula, Moctoby, Mongolic, Taensa and the Ouachita to name a few. Altogether there were about 30 tribes, some of whom were friendly and some who were not. They lived by hunting, fishing, stealing anything they could get their hands on – and, of course, killing white men or fighting with other tribes.

You never knew what mood the river would be in – many lives had been taken by the Mississippi but it had also provided a living for many people and they loved the river. Many countries had tried to claim it – Spain, France and England being amongst them – and the riverbanks had seen many battles over the years. But there would only ever be one owner of the river – the river itself. The mouth of the river and the surrounding area was under the French flag. There was fresh water on the inside of the mouth of the river and ships would fill up with fresh water whilst loading and unloading. The French called the river Myssysypy and spelt it this way. The French travelled down the Mississippi from Canada right down to New Orleans. The mouth of the Mississippi was 3800 km of twisting, bending, rough, smooth, fast, slow, hot and cold waters. She was dangerous, deep, shallow, clear and muddy and if she could talk – what stories she would have to tell. Her riverbanks were inhabited by Indians, settlers, buffalo, deer, rabbits, rats, snakes and many more and the river by fish and crocodiles. These were all the things Red Burlington knew and loved about the river.

In the Gulf of Mexico ships traded from all over Europe with all kinds of cargo but the waters were also plagued pirates, many of whom became legends – Captain Morgan, Black Beard and many others. Spanish galleons from New Orleans carried fortunes on board – gold, silver, coins, fine clothes and wine and would often be attacked by pirates when they were sailing back to Spain. The pirates were aware of every ship loading and unloading and knew the cargoes they were carrying so that when they set sail the pirates would be out at sea waiting. They would attack and kill the crew, take the cargo and sink the ship. They would then sail away to smaller islands along the coast to hide and sell their cargo. To try to stop this happening, Spain decided to send war ships to the Gulf in order to make the seaways safe. Some of the war ships carried ten guns.

The pirates knew Red Burlington's ship, her cargo and the date she was due to set sail and by the end of the ten days *The Pretender* was loaded and ready to sail. Red Burling was not only a good captain, he was also well known for his navigational skills. Many times he had been asked to pilot a boat down the river and now he was leaving the river heading out to the open sea. It wasn't the first time he had done this and every time he left the river he immediately started to look forward to coming back. His journey this time was to New Orleans; down to St Petersburg; Havana, Cuba; Nassau, the West Indies; Cat Island; Kingston, Jamaica then over to Galveston. He had been to the West Indies as a first mate some years back so he knew the journey. Red had studied everything about sailing ships – the sea, winds, trade, currents, weather signs; it was his life, it was his love. Red could recognise a ship even before anyone saw the ship's flag. He would know which ship it was and this had saved his ship and the lives of his crew more than once. He could tell if it was a pirate ship and as his ship had many guns he would order his crew to be prepared for battle. When the pirate ship came alongside ready to board, Red would order the crew to open fire, killing many pirates.

Red told his bosun that they would be dropping anchor at Dauphine Bay as he had work to do before they hit open water and told him not to say anything to anyone. A day later they dropped anchor at Dauphine Bay and Red instructed his crew to break open the crates as quickly as they could. The first four cases had big guns. "No wonder they were heavy," said the bosun. Red told them he wanted two portside mid-ship and two starboard mid-ship. Gun doors had already been cut into the ship and Red told them to get them into position and tie down the other two crates. These contained shot, powder and balls poles. "Hurry, men, I don't want to be seen and want to be underway as soon as we can," shouted Red. It was heavy work getting the guns into position and tied down but it was done in six hours and as they set sail Red thought to himself, "Now let's see a pirate."

As if testing *The Pretender* they hit a storm three days out to sea, but she was ready and she proved it. For almost two days she rode the storm and at the end Red Burlington said to his crew, "She is beautiful – what a ship! She feels alive. The ship and I are one – I live for her and she lives for me. I feel she will look after us. It's as if she is talking to me. I feel like I have been waiting all my life for her and she knows it."

Even the crew felt something – they didn't know what it was but it felt good.

It was a good run down to Nassau. They had good strong winds and hot weather, they hadn't seen any pirates and Red had been able to get a lot of work done – more than he had hoped. If this trip went well, the McCoil family had told him that *The Pretender* would be all his for as long as he wanted; to be her captain and that was all he wanted. Eight of the crew had sailed with Red before – the bosun, the ship's cook, the chippy, old Joe One Hand, three deck hands and an old negro called Kassy Belagonaa. He never used his name and had always been knows as Pepper Pot. The story goes that he got this name because when he was a young boy living on a cotton plantation along the Mississippi River, he was helping the cook to make a large meal of stew in an extra large cooking pot. He accidentally knocked a big bag of black pepper into the stew and when the plantation workers came in to eat, the stew was so hot they all ran down to the river and drunk the Mississippi dry. They had to wait for the rain to come before the river would flow again. He never told anyone about the bag of black pepper as he was too scared. When Red first heard this story he told Pepper Pot that before he ate any food he would make him test it first. Pepper Pot's job on the ship was to work in the galley and help on deck when they were in port. He was a lovely old man and no one had a bad word to say against him. In the evenings, when the crew were changing the ship's sails, old Pepper Pot would sit up on deck and play for them. He had a home made banjo – if that's what you could call it – but it played beautiful music and every night the crew would ask him to play and sing. One of their favourite songs was called *Benjamin Bee*, a song about a Negro who worked on a cotton plantation on the riverbank, and when he could he would sit on a tree branch and fish, but one day he fell in. Here's how it went:

Old Benjamin Bee

Benjamin Bee fell out of a tree into the Mississippi
Now the Mississippi is wild and free and took away old Benjamin Bee

CHORUS:
You could hear him cry
Lordy lordy, you could hear him cry
Lordy, lordy, I don't want to die
Lordy lordy, I don't want to die
Lordy lordy, I don't want to cry
Benjamin Bee, Benjamin Bee

There's fish on the hook, bread on the ground
But old Benjamin Bee is nowhere to be found
The cotton is high, the land is dry
Without Benjamin Bee we will all die
Benjamin Bee, Benjamin Bee

You could hear him cry
Lordy lordy, I don't want to die
Lordy lordy, I don't want to cry
Lordy lordy, I don't want to cry
Lordy lordy, I don't want to die
Benjamin Bee Benjamin Bee

Mississippi you're wild and free
Give me back that belongs to me
They say when the sun is out of the sky
And the old grey wolf goes hurrying by

You can hear him cry
Lordy lordy, I don't want to die
Benjamin Bee, Benjamin Bee

You could hear him cry
Lordy lordy, I don't want to die
Lordy lordy, I don't want to cry
Lordy lordy, I don't want to cry
Lordy lordy, I don't want to die
Benjamin Bee Benjamin Bee

The crew love it and every time the chorus came round, they sang their heads off and even Red joined in. Pepper Pot said the music came from the negros in the South; it was called 'the Blues' and there was also a poem of Benjamin Bee.

Benjamin Bee, Benjamin Bee fell out of a tree
Fell into the Mississippi that took him to sea
He still had his hook, he still had his line
Don't you believe it, they were both mine

Pepper Pot used to say that he had once met Benjamin Bee's son who said that Benjamin used to fish up an old tree that used to lean out over the Mississippi. Benjamin would climb out as far as he could to have more chance of catching fish. He must have caught a fish and as he was climbing down the tree, he slipped and fell in because all they found was a fish on a hook at the bottom of the tree. The crew would laugh at Pepper Pot and walk away. No one knew for sure if he was telling the truth, but he came from the same part of the river as Benjamin Bee. Even Red wouldn't say whether it was true or not – all he would say is that Pepper Pot knew the truth.

In Red's cabin was a small table stacked high with charts, maps and an old compass, and his sea route all mapped out. After leaving the Mississippi *The Pretender*'s first port of call was

St Petersburg, crossing the Gulf of Mexico, where she would unload most of her cargo, reload and set sail to Havana, Cuba. The she would pick up the winds from the Florida Straits that would take her to Nassau in the West Indies. Then on to Cat Island for supplies. Then sail on to Haiti, through the windward passage, to pick up the Cuba Greater Antilles sea that would take them down to Kingston, Jamaica. Then onto their last port of call, through the Yucatan Channel, back into the Gulf of Mexico and across to Galveston, where the McCoils had a trading centre where most of their goods were sold.

The McCoil family used to use whatever ship they could to move their goods – sometimes they had to wait months for a ship only to lose it all to pirates. With their own ship and captain they could move their goods all in one go whenever they wanted. That's why Major McCoil was so happy when he got his letter – his very own sailing ship, which would be anchored at the mouth of the Mississippi, under French law. The French had built a fort here and a small town – known today as New Orleans. France and the United States of America were working hard together to stop England and Spain getting a foothold in America.

The pirates worked in the islands of the West Indies, attacking sailing ships of any flag and choosing any one of the many islands to hide. This was the reason Red Burlington had four heavy guns put on board *The Pretender*. Once they sailed to the West Indies, the pirates could attack whenever they wanted.

Two hours after leaving Dauphine Island the bosun went to see the captain in his cabin. "That was a clever move, Captain, taking on three extra men. You're no fool," he said.

"There's an old saying," said the captain. "A fool and his money are soon parted and I don't intend to lose my ship."

The bosun asked the captain who would be doing what if they had to take the pirates on. The captain told him that the three extra men had all manned guns before and had all served on war ships. The bosun was pleased to hear this and he left the captain to study his maps.

At the start of the voyage *The Pretender* had made slow progress but the captain made her go faster. She could cut the wind quicker than most ships and the crew got to know everything they could about her so that if anything were to go wrong they would know what to do. The captain also taught them how to fight off a pirate attack. To any pirate ship *The Pretender* looked like a cargo-carrying sailing ship, as the captain intended, and so nothing happened on *The Pretender's* first voyage.

When they reached Kingston, Jamaica, Red Burlington went ashore to look around. Whilst walking through the streets an old witch doctor came up to him carrying a ritual drum stick. He shook this at Red and spoke to him of the ship of black and red and warned him that these were the colours of the dead, and with that he walked quickly away. There are many voodoo witch doctors in Jamaica. Jamaican people believe in voodoo, which it is said can bring pain and death, but Red Burlington just took it as another way of trying to get money out of him, even though the witch doctor had disappeared without asking for any. Red went into a nearby tavern, ordered some food and drink and sat at a table by the tavern window. Whilst he was eating, a black face that had been painted white suddenly appeared at the window, then just as suddenly it disappeared. Red wondered if this was the witch doctor he had seen earlier.

Red Burlington was captain of *The Pretender* for 36 years. It was a long time for a captain to stay with one ship. He had lost count of how many voyages he had sailed on her but he had loved every minute and would do it all over again. At the beginning, she was attacked many times by pirates and buccaneers in the West Indies but because of her guns other ships would sail with her because they felt they would be better protected from the pirates. It wasn't long before the pirates and buccaneers learned of *The Pretender* and her captain and for a long time they left her alone. But on her second to last trip with Red Burlington, she was attacked. Red was very badly injured when the pirates tried to board *The Pretender* but single handed he fought off ten pirates, killing four. The fifth had a broken neck. Three were so badly beaten they would be lucky if they lived. The ninth fell on his own dagger and the tenth was thrown overboard. Red Burlington had six knife wounds, had been beaten with a pole, he was covered in blood but at 65 years old he was still a very powerful man and could still put up a good fight, as the pirates found out. The pirates had lost more men in their battle with Red Burlington's crew then they had in their last five attacks and the ones that survived retreated. Red had lost so much blood and had been so badly injured it looked like he might die, but his crew nursed him night and day whilst successfully sailing the boat back to New Orleans, by which time Red had recovered.

When *The Pretender* returned from its first voyage, a week earlier than expected, Morgan and Lucy McCoil were waiting ashore to greet their captain and crew. Red Burlington told them that the gods must have been looking after them. Once all the details of the voyage and the cargo had been discussed, Morgan gave Red a pocket watch and told him that his father had intended to give this to him on his return from his first voyage. His father was happy not only to have his ship but to have found the best person to be her captain. "*The Pretender*'s yours, Captain Burlington, for as long as you want to sail her," said Morgan.

"Thank you, Mr McCoil," said Red. "It is a great honour to be captain of *The Pretender* and my crew and I will serve you well for many years to come."

The shook hands and a bond was made.

Lucy McCoil turned the watch over in Red's hand and showed him the inscription on the back. It said:

May she forever sail the seas
To Red Burlington, captain of 'The Pretender'
From Major Cane McCoil
In the year 1702

After reading this, Red went to speak but Lucy put her hand on Red's arm and said "God bless" and with that Lucy and Morgan walked away.

All through the years that Red was captain of *The Pretender* he flew the black flag at all times and at six every evening the ship's bell was rung. It was One Hand Joe's job to ring the bell, which he did until he died in 1711. Pepper Pot died the following year. In 1735 the bosun had been killed fighting off pirates, the chippy dropped dead and Red had lost a lot of crew fighting off pirates, but there were always seamen who wanted to sail with him.

It was not until 1711 that Red found out that the pirates had pledged 50 gold pieces to the first man to capture the black flag. A pirate ship had tried to come alongside starboard side but Red had opened two guns on them and the ship went down with nearly all hands. It was one of the pirates they had pulled out of the sea who told Red about the 50 gold pieces. By the 1740s, pirates and buccaneers were almost over and the seas were safe again. Pirates like Black Beard had been caught and hung, Captain Kid had died, Henry Morgan had become governor and most of the small unknown pirates were either dead or in jail.

Red had been at anchor for two weeks waiting for details of his new cargo and his orders for the next voyage, when he set sail for Havana, Cuba. During the voyage, Captain Burlington was taken ill – all those years of fighting and drinking and the hard life at sea had caught up with him and he knew this would be his last trip. He gave a letter to a captain he knew who was sailing to New Orleans and asked him to pass it on to Morgan

McCoil. When *The Pretender* sailed into New Orleans, Morgan and Lucy came aboard. "You have taken a great deal of worry off our minds, Captain," said Morgan. "I'm afraid I have some sad news for you. It has been very hard to find cargo for you on your last two trips as the Bolton trading companies are taking all our trade. I have had to sell all the businesses and *The Pretender*, because if I carry on I will lose a lot of money. We are moving to Jackson but in view of your very long and faithful service, we would like to give you 10,000 gold coins. With this you will be able to live a very good life anywhere you want; you will be a very rich man."

"But what is going to happen to the ship?" Red asked.

"I had hoped you wouldn't ask me that," said Morgan. "I'm sorry to say I think she is going to be berthed at the Grange."

"But that is the dirtiest, filthiest place in New Orleans," said Red, "it's where prostitutes live and cut-throats, drugs and the lowest of the low hang out. What will they use her for?"

Morgan hung his head as he told Red that he thought it was going to be used as a floating brothel. In that one short sentence Red Burlington's world fell apart. He felt dead inside and everything about him was screaming NO! He could hear *The Pretender* shouting "help me, help me, I'll die of shame, please don't let this happen to me, help me". Then he heard Morgan McCoil saying that he had tried to get her sold to the trading companies but they said she was too old and too small.

"When do you think you can hand her over," Morgan asked Captain Red.

"It will take about two weeks," he replied.

"That's fine," said Morgan. "I will say it will be ready by the 21st of the month."

They talked for a little while more before Lucy and Morgan McCoil left *The Pretender* for the last time as a very sad captain walked her decks.

In the following two weeks Red thought of nothing else until he finally knew what he had to do. He got his old crew together and told them of his plan and they were all for it, so on the night before she was due to be taken away, at the dead of night, *The Pretender* slipped her moorings and slowly and silently slipped away out to sea.

What was going on in Red Burlington's mind, no one knew, but we do know that if he had been caught he would have been charged with stealing a cargo sailing ship and could have been hung or imprisoned for a very long time. From that night on *The Pretender* was never seen again. Where the captain went and what he did we will never know. And what about his crew? What happened to them? They, the ship and Red Burlington were never seen again in this world.

Red Burlington and Major McCoil were very much alike in a lot of ways; they both liked a fight – Major McCoil in and out of the army and Red in and out of bars; both had only one love – Burlington's first and only love died and Major McCoil met and married his first and only love; both worked and lived on or by the Mississippi river and both loved the Sea. McCoil once said to Burlington that his only dream was to sail on *The Pretender*. In the short time they had known each other they had become good friends and when McCoil died in front of Red on the deck of *The Pretender* it was a great shock to him. He had found and lost a friend in a very short space of time and for the next 35 years he had kept his promise to fly the black flag, which had become *The Pretender's* trademark, known all over the West Indies and the Caribbean. Even though Major McCoil asked the captain to call him Cane, Red Burlington always called him Major and Major McCoil always called Burlington Red. Because of the difference in their heights it didn't take long for jokes to be made about them. People would ask "do you want a long one or a short one" or "shall I go the long way round, no go the shortest". These jokes would always be made loud enough so that they could both hear them. The best one of all was once when McCoil and Red were out walking and Red said to McCoil, "I'll pick the apples from the top of the tree and you can pick the apples off the ground. It will be quicker that way and it will save you jumping up and down." They always used to laugh whenever they heard these jokes. It didn't stop them from trying to help anyone who asked, either with money or power from McCoil or power and fists from Red.

Was it fate that brought them together for such a short time? Red often thought about the witch doctor who stopped him in Jamaica and the words the witch doctor said sometimes played on his mind:

Beware of the ship that carries the flag of black and red
For it is the colours of the dead

When Major McCoil had the inscription done on the back of the watch to give to Red his whole being went into every word. He was so proud of *The Pretender* and he wanted her to sail the seas forever. He wanted the world to see her, it was his dream come true. From a very small boy he had wanted a sailing ship. He dreamt of standing on the fo'c'sle deck looking seaward with a captain who looked just like Red Burlington. Had the words on the watch come true? Was it possible that in another dimension *The Pretender* with Captain Burlington and his crew were still sailing the seas? Seeing *The Pretender* was a sign of victory – the good always beating the bad.

Here are a few stories told down through the years of *The Pretender*.

In 1941 a German U-boat picked out a British merchant ship. It was 3,000 yards away but the captain of the U-boat wanted to get closer. Looking through his periscope they approached. At 2,500 yards he looked away; he looked back again at 2,000 yards and in front of the merchant ship was an old cargo sailing ship. "Where the hell did that come from?" he said. Them he was told by one of his first officers that two destroyers had left the convoy and were heading straight for them. The captain stood deep in thought as he wasn't sure what to do.

"Captain, the destroyers," his first officer shouted. Jumping into action, the captain ordered, "Fire one tube and let's get out of here." Suddenly they were hit by their own torpedo. Although the torpedo had been heading straight for the sailing ship and the merchant ship, it had made a u-turn and hit the sub. A nearby US destroyer, *Richmond,* picked up the U-boat crew and was told by the German captain that he had seen a sailing ship flying a black flag with a big man at the helm and a smaller man on the fo'c'sle, sailing side by side with the British merchant ship, and then it suddenly disappeared. The captain of the *Richmond* just looked at him and told him to go below and put on some dry clothes.

In 1943 a US destroyer was patrolling the North Atlantic when a thick heavy mist came down. The captain ordered slow ahead. After about five minutes the lookout came onto the bridge and told the captain that there had been a break in the fog and he had seen an old sailing ship with a big man standing at the wheel and a smaller man in a blue uniform on the fo'c'sle. "It was flying a black flag," he said.

At this the captain jumped up out of his chair and pressed the action stations button. Suddenly the fog lifted and there in front of them lying dead ahead was the mighty German battleship *Kisenburg.* "Open Fire," shouted the captain and before the *Kisenburg* had a chance to return fire she was hit many times and sunk to the bottom of the ocean.

Later that evening when the captain and his officers were having their dinner, the ship's doctor was just about to say something to the captain when he put his hands up to silence everyone. "Gentlemen," he said, "I want to tell you a story. When I got command of my first US destroyer it was called

The Mississippi, and I decided to find out as much as I could about her namesake, the Mississippi River, so I went to the library and got lots of books out. I read about the river its people, the old town called New Orleans, the ships that called there and at the end of one book I read a story about a sailing ship called *The Pretender*. *The Pretender* flew under a black flag and whenever people see it at sea, it's a warning that there is danger ahead. As soon as the lookout said that the ship he saw was flying a black flag, I knew we were in some kind of danger, that's why I pressed the action stations button. How do I know it's true, I hear you ask. Well, I have a friend who is the captain of the destroyer *Richmond* and he told me a similar story about the sailing boat and a German U-boat. So," said the captain, "let's us raise a toast to *The Pretender* for saving our lives."

In 1740 a small cargo sailing boat was under attack by a pirate ship. As the pirate boat got ready to board one of the pirates shouted a warning that *The Pretender* was heading straight for them. As *The Pretender* was too powerful for them, the pirates sailed away leaving the small cargo boat and its crew to safely go on their way. The story the pirates told afterwards was that one minute *The Pretender* was heading straight for them and the next minute it was gone. The cargo boat crew also said that they saw *The Pretender* chasing the pirate ship and then suddenly it disappeared.

Down through the years *The Pretender* has been seen many times but only when there is danger. Some say that a U-boat had the *Queen Mary* in her sights and was ready to torpedo her but the captain, looking through his periscope, lost sight of the *Queen Mary* and all he could see was an old sailing ship flying a black flag. He turned away shaking his head and when he looked back the sailing ship had gone and the *Queen Mary* was far away, together with the 1,000 troops on board. It was also said that Nelson's lookout reported seeing the sailing ship before the Battle of the Nile.

One old sailor whose ship went down said he had been in the water for a long time when he saw an old sailing ship coming towards him, but it sailed on by. He watched it sail away and when he looked round he saw a large raft. The raft saved his life but he never knew where the sailing ship went.

And so the stories go on about The Pretender, Red Burlington and Major McCoil. Let's hope they never stop.

The Last Page

In 1960 Dazon Lawrence was 20 years old, and that was the year his grandmother died. Being her only grandchild she left him all her money, £10,000, and left her big old house to his mother and father. At that time Dazon was working for a small antiques company and he loved his job. He had read many books on antiques and owned a large collection; he loved old furniture and vases and knew a great deal on both. He told his father that with the money he was going to open an antique shop, but first he needed to buy stock.

A month later Dazon opened his small shop and he put a board outside saying 'now open – will buy antiques, good price given'. In his first week he bought and sold many antiques and added another sign outside which read 'will call at your home to buy and collect antiques'. The telephone did not stop ringing and in his second week he told his father that he would need to hire an assistant as he could not do everything on his own, "There is just too much to do." he said. The very next day a young girl of about 20-25 came into his shop to sell two old Chinese vases. As soon as Dazon saw them he knew that they were worth a lot of money and he liked the girl, whose name was Sally. "I don't know for sure what they're worth but what I will do is give you £200 for them now and if you call back in a week I will know more about them and their value. If they are what I think they are, I'll give you more money." – Sally agreed. Then Dazon asked her if she happened to be looking

67

for a job, to which she replied "Yes I am, that's why I'm selling these vases,"

"How would you like to work here, in my shop?"

"That would be wonderful!"

"When can you start?"

"When do you need me?"

"Today? Tell you what, come back at one o'clock and start work and I will pay you a full day's wages"

That was the start of a short courtship and a long, happy marriage that produced one son. Within three years he was married to Sally and had opened another four shops, and because he was honest, fair and well-liked within the antiques industry, he made a great deal of money. Five years later he had a son and had been married for four and a half years – he had married Sally within six months of their first meeting.

Soon it was 1965 and his son's fourth birthday, and by 1985 Dazon had antique shops all over England as well as in Paris, Rome, New York, Sydney and Canada; he was worth £8,000,000,000 and of the number of people he had working for him he had no idea. As soon as his son (who they named Calmon) could walk and talk Dazon began to teach him about antiques, and when Calmon was 24 years old he knew almost as much as his father about the antique trade. Calmon was sent all over the world buying and selling and was as well known and liked as his father. Calmon was not married but had a girlfriend of around six months called Anna – Calmon had no intention of marrying until he was around 30 years old.

It was just another antiques sale that his father had asked him to go to in Bedford, Dazon had said to him "there is a lot of furniture up for auction – buy the lot, whatever the cost". So Calmon went to Bedford and to the auction where he caused a stir by buying all of the furniture and after the auction he visited a small gallery full of paintings that were also up for sale. Here he saw an oil painting of a young girl of about twenty years old, the painting was of her face and she was beautiful although her slight smile had a touch of evil in it. She had long brown hair which reached her shoulders and her eyes were soft one minute and hard the next. As soon as Calmon saw her he knew he had to buy her and noting the asking price of £5000 he bought the painting and took it back to his hotel. The only names on the painting were those of the artist – Herze Vehiden – and the name of a village, Berger Gann, in Germany. Calmon put the painting in his suitcase and went down to the restaurant to eat. That night he had a few drinks and it had passed midnight by the time he returned to his room where he undressed, fell on his bed and slept until eight o'clock the next morning. At breakfast he remembered a dream he had had about the girl from the painting, she had come to his bed where they had made love all night, it was so real but he blamed the amount of drink he had consumed the night before. But, there was one strange thing that Calmon could not dismiss as a dream – that morning his pillow had smelt of a beautiful perfume that he had not smelt before. Could a girl come out of a painting and make love to him all night? For the next few days he could not get the dream out if his head – was it really a dream or could it be real?

Calmon searched everywhere but he could not find any record of a Herze Vehiden and so he decided that he would go over to Germany to see what he could discover. The next day he flew out to Germany and hired a car which he drove to Berger Gann, taking the painting with him. He went into an art shop that sold paints, paintings and drawing kits and he asked the shop owner about Herze Vehiden. The shop owner became very angry when this name was mentioned and Calmon was asked to leave the shop and never go back as he would not be welcome. As soon as he left the art shop the owner pulled down the blinds and locked the door. Calmon went to the local library and looked through old records, still finding no mention of Herze Vehiden and when he asked the librarian he was once again told to leave and not return.

While Calmon took a walk around the small town he noticed that he was being followed by a small, fat man. The man followed him all the way back to his hotel but carried on past as Calmon went inside. That night he had a meal at the hotel followed by some drinks at the bar where he stayed until early morning. When he awoke the next day he found a large brown envelope had been pushed under his door, Calmon opened it to find approximately 10 sheets of A4 paper typed in English, he looked through to see if he could find out who had delivered the envelope but there was no name, there was nothing at all and when he rang reception to enquire as to whether anyone had asked for his room number he was told "no". Calmon had just sat down to read the mysterious typed sheets when the phone rang and it was his father calling about an auction in Liverpool which he could not attend as Calmon's mother was ill, "Can you go instead?" Dazon wanted to know.

"When is it?"

"Friday the 8th, starts at 10 o'clock at the Stamford hotel. I will book you a room for three nights as the auction is on for two days. There will be a list at reception of everything I want you to buy".

Dazon and his father spoke for a further half and hour and when they said their goodbyes Calmon finally sat down with the typed papers, he picked up the first sheet.

Page One

The Countess Cenareka Rasomoa Von-Bassingor born 1747, died 1767 in the village of Berger Gann, the first daughter of Count and Countess Von-Bassingor of Vossing Castle. Count Von-Bassingor was very rich and powerful and owned a great amount of land in and around Berger Gann. The young Countess Cenareka had a sister, Caneka, who died at the age of 6 and a brother, Mikoff, who died at the age of 10. Mikoff, they said, was insane and they had locked him up in one of the towers, he escaped but fell over a balcony to his death.

Page Two

It was said that the Countess Cenareka was sex mad and took many lovers, with her first being a stable boy when she was 10 years old. The stable boy was later found with a hay fork in his chest. At 6 years old it had become obvious that Cenareka had an evil streak, if anybody got in her way she would beat them with her riding whip, she would beat the villagers merely for fun and by the time she was fifteen years old and had taken over a thousand lovers, including officers from her father's army, every one was either found dead or never seen again. Wherever the Countess went, a man named Gormo went with her, he was 6 foot 7 inches tall, weighed twenty-eight stone, and he had a gammy right leg and rode a large black cart horse.

Page Three

Gormo never let Cenareka out of his sight; if anybody got too close he would hit them with the heavy staff that he carried on his horse, with a long thick horse whip or with a long, broad sword. Around his waist he carried a long, sharp hunting knife. He never spoke, they said that he could but he suffered from a debilitating stutter, he had an ugly face, almost square and he had long black hair that reached down past his shoulders. More than once he had whipped a farm hand to death for getting too close to the Countess and the people hated them both, they wished both Cenareka and her body guard dead but were too frightened of them to do anything about it. The Count's soldiers were stationed all around the village watching all that occurred and so no meetings or gatherings were possible. Nobody ever saw the Count and his wife so the army ruled the village and the villagers, who had very hard and unhappy lives.

Page Four

There was only one man who saw the Count and Countess regularly. The Count loved looking at paintings and Herze Vehiden was a painter (a very good one too) who lived in the village and earned a decent living from his art work. The Count heard of him by reputation from his Captain of the Guard and so called Herze Vehiden to his castle asking him to create a painting of his favourite horse. The moment the Count saw the finished product he recognised Herze Vehiden as a great and gifted painter and set him to paint his wife, himself, his garden, his castle, the river, the bridge and his soldiers and through the process of his work the artist gathered a great deal of information about the workings of the castle and the army. He discovered that at some point in the near future much of the Count's army was being dispatched to guard the land borders many miles away, leaving only a small platoon of soldiers to watch over the village. In total the artist painted twenty-two oil paintings for the Count but he had never been asked to paint the young Countess until one day she called for him herself requesting two portraits – one of her head and shoulders and the other of her full body, "you will be called to begin soon", she said, "have your paints and brushes ready. Be warned that if I do not like what I see I will have you hanged in the village".

Page Five

Even though large gatherings were not permitted the villagers managed to get together in small groups, taking it in turns to go to different houses. They were very careful about doing this because they knew that if they were found they would be tortured and hanged – as would their families but they were relying on Herze Vehiden to tell them everything he knew about life inside the castle walls. The artist, just like the villagers, despised the Count, his wife and the evil Countess

Cenareka Rasomoa Von-Bassingor who was now nineteen years old and would set fire to the villager's houses at night. Families would be lucky to survive Cenareka's wicked games and she would laugh at their despair. She would set fire to the hay stacks that had been laboured over in the fields and in a particularly viscous act she ran over a little girl whilst riding her horse at great speed through the village. For this she was unapologetic – merely commenting, "That's one brat less to feed". On hearing Herze Vehiden tell of the plan to relocate the Count's army the villagers decided that it was time to do something about the evil Countess. As soon as the soldiers left for the border they would overthrow the platoon that was left and then hunt down the young Countess Cenareka who they would hang and set fire to. There would be nothing left of Countess Cenareka Rasomoa Von-Bassingor. Once she was dead they would do the same to her mother and father, they would release all of the prisoners from the castle dungeons and finally raise the castle to the ground. They had other plans for Gormo – they would tie him to a post and make him watch his mistress hang, then they would burn him alive before cutting off his head- but in the mean time they just needed to sit and wait and make plans until they were given the word by Herze Vehiden.

Page Six
Count Von-Bassingor had come into power thirty years before after his father had had poison placed in his wine, and he had since ruled with a rod of iron. The dungeons were full, there were hangings almost everyday, there were village square whippings for any reason whatsoever and his sex-mad, evil, insane daughter loved nothing more than to hurt people, the Countess did whatever she wanted, whenever she wanted and if for any reason she did not get her own way the villagers would pay the price. Cenareka would laugh one minute and beat you the next and everybody in the village was frightened

of her violent moods, she could drink any man under the table which would cause her raw evil to surface and she would want to fight anyone. You would always let her win, if you didn't Gormo would be ordered to put his hunting knife across your throat – in short, to live, you lost. Any man she desired she had to have, it did not matter who he was and if he refused Gormo was instructed to whip them and remove them. Most times the man in question was never seen again. But little did the Countess know that her time was running out! Born on the black Tuesday of April 19th 1747 she died on the black Tuesday of 19th April 1767, born evil she died evil. It was said that the devil was there at her hanging – waiting.

Page Seven

A week after calling Herze Vehiden to be ready with his paints the Countess requested that he begin painting her and when the artist arrived Cenareka was lying naked on a large bed. After eight sittings the painting was finished and the young Countess loved what she saw but she told the painter that he should not tell anyone about his work – she took the painting and he never saw it again, although he heard that she gave it to her trusted, faithful servant Gormo. Vehiden was then ordered to paint her head and shoulders only and so he set to work but whilst painting this second portrait he felt evil surround him and he lost all consciousness of his work. He said later "I don't remember painting her – I would start and then the next thing I know I am cleaning my brushes, and then at the end, after 5 sittings I looked at the painting properly for the very first time. Looking at her scared me to death, she had a slight evil smile on that beautiful face; she could have been the devil's daughter". Was that why the devil was at her hanging, was he waiting for her to come home? He knew deep down that it was not him who painted the Countess but something evil. The devil himself maybe? Then finally, Herze Vehiden heard that the army were moving to the border a week later, he shared this information with the villagers and also told them of the paintings of the Countess, "we must destroy them in the fire with her" he told them. So for the next week the villagers got out their bows, swords, staffs and knives ready for what they were calling 'Freedom Day'.

Page Eight

The villagers watched the army march off a week later and waited two long days before launching their attack – knowing that by this time the soldiers were too far away to get back to stop them. On the third day, early in the morning they launched their attack on the remaining guards who surrendered quickly, laying down their arms and offering to join the villagers in their uprising. They found Cenareka and Gormo in the stables, Gormo put up a brave fight but there were too many against him and they threw nets over him and put heavy chains on him. They chained the Countess and took her away for a quick trial for which she was found guilty of her crimes against the villagers and sentenced to hanging. The gallows were ready for use with a huge amount of wood piled high around them ready to be set on fire. They took her screaming to her death. A large crowd gathered at the gallows shouting at her and throwing rotten vegetables at her, they tried to get at her as she stood at the gallows, but as they slipped the rope over her neck she smiled and cried out "On this day I will curse you and this village for all time. All first born baby boys will die within their first year – all of them from insanity and all first born baby girls will die of boils, ulcers and scabs again within their first year. It will go on and on until this village is dead!" The villagers shouted back at her, "burn the witch, burn the evil witch" they chanted. For thirty years, since the Count had taken power in the village the villagers had waited for this day, the day they could begin to live in peace. The village elder put his hands in the air and everybody quietened, "Go to hell Countess" he said and pulled the trap door open, she fell through the wood and her neck was broken, the village doctor called out to the waiting crowd "She is dead!"

Page Nine

They found only one painting of the Countess, the naked portrait was found in Gormo's room and thrown onto the fire and the villagers headed into the castle taking everything they could. The Count and his wife saw them coming and saw that they were carrying swords, staffs, knives and whips and knew that they would be killed and so they filled their wine glasses with strong poison – when the villagers reached them they were already dead. Returning to the gallows the fire was roaring and suddenly the villagers heard a loud scream which gave way to an evil laughter so scary that people got on their hands and knees to pray to god to protect them. The fire burned for many hours, it roared high into the sky and when it finally burnt out the villagers looked through the ashes to collect the Countess's bones but they could find nothing of her. Gormo was chained by the remains of the great fire – suddenly a woman ran towards him and plunged a knife into his heart, "you killed my baby" she screamed as she was helped away and Gormo's body was thrown onto the ashes. For a while life was good for the villagers, they started to sing and to dance and the children played games, running around safe and happy but then the first new babies were born and they all died within their first year – the boys of insanity and the girls of boils, ulcers and scabs. The Countess's curse was working and the villagers began to move away – far away from the village where the curse could no longer touch them but of those that stayed, their children and their children's children continued to carry the curse. It is only since doctors developed cures for these conditions that the curse has been able to die out. Old Herze Vehiden died five years later. How he died nobody knows but they found him sitting by a half finished painting with his mouth open in an expression of shock – as if something had frightened him to death. It is said that if he had not painted the Countess the curse would never have happened.

Page Ten

So you see my friend why I tell you this story. The painting has not been seen for over three hundred years, it is evil my friend and people will kill you because they do not want the curse to start up again in this village. You must destroy it as soon as you can for not only are you in danger of the villagers but also of the painting – I do not wish to see you die. Your hotel bill has been paid and you must leave tomorrow morning, there is a plane ticket back to England waiting for you. Germany will always welcome you but do not come back here, if you do not leave tomorrow by the end of the day you will be dead.

Calmon looked at his watch, it was three o'clock in the morning and on ringing reception it was confirmed that his bill had been paid and his plane ticket was ready. The story had to be true and he had to get out of the village as soon as possible, yes, he would be on that plane today. At eight o'clock that morning Calmon left to drive to the airport and as he looked back at the hotel he saw two men, watching him drive away.

Back home Calmon kept quiet about the painting and the story but a week later he decided to tell his father everything, he showed Dazon the painting and let him read the story. "Son, you are in big trouble", said Dazon, "you must get rid of the painting, lets go into the garden, build a bonfire and destroy the painting for if you ever have children – need I say more?" However, there was a part of the story that Calmon did not know.

Last Page

Do not burn the painting, take it to your church and let your priest say a prayer over it then have him sprinkle it with holy water. Take the painting home and pour more holy water over it and you will see the Countess's face disappear, once this has happened place a bible and cross on the frame and very soon there will be nothing of the painting left, only then will it be safe to burn the canvas and the frame. If you burn the painting whilst looking at the Countess's face she will see you and she will kill you – you will be the last person to be cursed.

Calmon knew nothing of this last page as it had fallen under his bed back at the hotel room in Berger Gann. It was discovered by the cleaning lady who entered his room later that day and not being able to read English she assumed it was rubbish and threw it away. Meanwhile Dazon had got a great fire blazing and Calmon threw the painting into the flames – as he did so a scream burst from the image of the Countess and Dazon turned to find his son lying dead on the ground.

Part Two

And the Angel Called Twice

Part One

John David Canbury was one of those men you would be lucky to bump into in your life. He was a gentle, caring, honest, loving man who never had a bad word for anybody and if you needed help he was there for you. He was liked by everybody, just went through life a happy man, not a care in the world. Good job, nice home he still lived at home with his parents, no money worries. Loved a pint and a game of darts; all he needed was a girl in his life. It was weekend time again and he was getting ready for a night up the local when he got a phone call that was to change his life forever. One of his mates was getting married and asked John to the wedding.

"Great thanks Pete look forward to it."

"Don't forget the stag night on the 20th at the Sailors Arms about 8'o clock."

"I'll be there."

"Okay see you."

And as I said that was the start of a new world, new life, new beginning - or the beginning of the end.

That was two years ago. Now he had a beautiful wife, a beautiful daughter he worshipped. He worshipped them both and he would always be fussing around them. You could say that he loved his wife beyond life itself. Where she went, he went and where he went she went, they did everything together. It was a match made in heaven for both of them.

He fell in love with his wife the first time he saw her. She was standing at a bus stop. Her name was Correna Cantel, she was part Spanish.

On that same day Correna told a friend, "I saw a man today at the bus stop that I'm going to marry some day!"

"How do you know? He might already be married."

"I don't know, I just know he's the man for me. He's lovely!"

So fate had stepped in. Round one.

On the following Saturday, John's friend was getting married and John was looking forward to it. Who else was going to the wedding? Correna Cantel. Round two.

So the 26th August was to be the start of two young people falling in love with one another; madly in love 'till death do us part'.

John went to the wedding with some friends and Correna went with her friends. It was a great wedding. There were so many people there that not everyone could get into the church for the service. It was after the service that guests were put into groups to have their photos taken. There were too many for one shot. John was in one group waiting for the photo to be taken, when he saw her and she saw him. He just looked at her and she at him. Then someone called his name - he turned to see who was calling him and when he looked back she was gone. He felt sick, ill. You name it he felt it for those few minutes. Where had she gone?

Then again his name was called, "John come over here you're in this group!" So John walked over to have his photo taken with a group waiting for him.

"You stand here John," his friend told poor John. He did not know if he was coming or going as he could not get the girl out of his mind. He looked to see who was standing next to him in the group and his heart stopped. God it was her! She was beautiful.

He knew he had fallen in love with this beautiful girl next to him. She smiled at him and said, "Hello John."

He replied almost in a whisper. "Hello back. I'm John."

"Yes I know," she told him. "I'm Correna."

They looked at each other and laughed.

"Can I buy you a drink after the photos?" he asked.

"Yes, I'd like that." So after many photos they walked off to the reception, which was held in a hall next to the church.

"How do you know my name?"

She laughed and said, "Michael Ray is your work mate?"

"Yes."

"Well, I know his wife Pat and she told me your name. We saw you on Paul's stag night and I asked her about you."

"Oh yes, and what else did she say about me?"

"Well you're not married, you're twenty-five, live at home, have a red car, been at Taylor's for six years and in September you will be the new manager. You are a good darts player in the local team, six foot tall and weigh about twelve and a half stone and have brown eyes. There I told you I know all about you!"

"But I know nothing about you! So now it's your turn."

"Well, my name is Correna Cantel I'm half Spanish, twenty years old, five foot four inches, eight and a half stone, grey eyes."

"Yes I had noticed," he told her.

"Single, no boyfriend and I live at home. I work for the bank in the high street." But what she didn't tell him was that she was like him, soft, loving, caring and gentle.

To tease her he said, "How do you know I have not got a girl friend?"

"You better not have!" Then she hit him playfully.

It was a great wedding, lots of food and drink, loud rock and roll music, but sad to say like all good things it had to come to an end. It was almost midnight time to go home.

On the way home Correna said, "This is the best day of my life, thank you for a lovely day."

"Thank you," John said.

It was nearly 1'o clock by the time he got her home and it was 3.30 in the morning before Correna said, "Look at the time, I've got to be up at 7am!" They had talked and talked and talked neither noticing the time.

"Can I see you again?" he asked.

"Yes. Tonight?"

"Yes."

It was nearly 4'o clock before she got out of the car.

"Look," he said, "I'm off work, I don't work Sundays. I'll drive you to work."

"Thank you. We are so short of staff that they asked me to work Sunday. Can't turn down money, this wedding cost me a fortune – a present, new dress..."

"Yes, I can see it shows a lot of you."

"Trust you..." she said. "Call for me at 8.30 - no make it 8am and have a cup of tea and meet my mum." She gave him a quick kiss then she was gone.

From that day on they saw each other every day. As I said, where she was he was and where he was she was.

It was almost a year to the day that they got married. It made you feel good and happy to watch them together for you could see the love they had for each other, a beautiful love. If she was not by his side he would look around for her and she would do the same. He would just smile and carry on talking to his friends, she would do the same. They were loved by so many people. She looked beautiful that day. He told a friend, "I've never seen a woman so beautiful in all my life than my wife. God I love her so!" They say love can make you look beautiful and it certainly did that day for Mrs Correna Canbury.

John's granddad died a short time after the wedding and left John £30,000 in his will. With his granddad's money they put a deposit on a house. Life for John and Correna was very good. John used to say, "If this is life can I have more please sir!" They both had good jobs, earned good money, were both fit and well and had many friends.

They had been married just over a year when Corre (as John called her) told him she was going to have a baby. "Wow!" John shouted and hugged and kissed his wife many times. And the next year Corre gave John a beautiful daughter they called her Melan'a after Corre's grandmother. She said, "You know I had it all planned to tell you that night we went to the Rainbow restaurant. I was going to wait until we finished our meal but I could not wait."

"I'm glad you didn't as I might have bought the whole restaurant a pint that night. Don't worry about money - I've got some good news to tell you too. I've been offered a partnership and my money goes up by a hundred pounds a week."

"I've got more news for you," she said. "I've been saving and I've just got £500 pound saved, plus mum gave us £1000."

So life for John and Corre was good. John told his father, "I'm a very lucky man, I've got a beautiful wife, daughter, lovely house and great job. What more can a man ask for?

"You know dad I've got more than I deserve, lots of men don't get a quarter out of life than I've got. Sometimes it frightens me!" "Don't be silly son enjoy what you've got. Only God can take it away from you, can you see him doing that? I don't think so. Go home, I've got work to do. I can't talk to you all day. Go home!"

They had been married now for almost seven years when one day John got home and found his wife in bed. She told John that she was washing up when she started to feel unwell so she got her mother to pick up Melane'a from school and went to bed. John called the doctor who said, "It looks like you wife has got a touch of flu - there is a lot going around at the moment. If you can get her to stay in bed for a few days the rest will do her good." And a few days later she was okay, up and about.

But a month later Corre was ill again, but worse than last time. Again John called the doctor in. "I don't like this. I think I'll send her for tests at Goodly hospital. I think it's more than flu this time, nothing to worry about, but I'm not taking any chances. Give her these twice a day they should help."

It was nearly three weeks before Corre was fit enough to go to hospital for the tests. The doctor told them, "It will take about five weeks to get the results back, just carry on as normal."

It was nearly six weeks when the doctor rang asking them to go and see him. "I've booked you in for Friday at 6'o clock. Is that okay?"

"Yes."

"Good. See you Friday." So Friday John and Corre sat in the doctors waiting room, not saying a word. John held Corre's hand. Eventually he whispered, "Don't worry darling everything will be fine, stop worrying." Then they heard their name called. The doctor, Doctor Holdworth was standing by the door.

"Come in take a seat. How are you feeling?"

"A little tired, lost some weight, I'm not eating or sleeping too well - otherwise okay."

"Good."

Corre looked at John who added, "Well, there is one more thing, Corre thinks her eyesight is going. Now and then her vision is blurred."

While John was talking the doctor was taking notes. "Well I've got the test results back. I'm sorry to tell you that they show you have terminal cancer. I'm very sorry to have to tell you. I've made an appointment for you on Monday to see a specialist, a Mr Rathan at 10'o clock at his surgery. Can you make it for Monday? Try not to worry - I'm sure Mr Rathan can tell you all you want to know and how to deal with any problems you come up against. I am very sorry to have to tell you this, but let's see what Mr Rathan has to say. As I said at this stage Mrs Canbury try not to worry. Let Mr Rathan do the worrying, that's his job. If at any time you want to see me just ring and I'll tell the receptionist to book you straight away."

"Can you not tell me any more?" she asked the doctor.

"Well Mr Rathan will go into full details of what treatment you can have and what it can do for you. Go home and try to enjoy your weekend."

On the way home they never said a word what could he say to her that night to not upset her more? But once they were home she fell into his arms and cried her eyes out. She cried like a little baby, there was nothing he could do for her but hold her in his arms, which he did for a long time.

It was a very long weekend waiting for Monday. They did not tell anybody, they wanted to wait until they had seen Mr Rathan. They stayed in all weekend on their own and many times Corre broke down. "Why me? Why me?" And again what could John say? He was so upset that he dare not speak as he knew he would break down - he had to be strong for her. But sometimes she wanted to talk so he let her talk, try to get some of the tension out of her body. It was a very sad weekend for both of them.

"I won't die will I? How long do you think I've got to live?" Questions like these she kept asking but what could he say? He did not know himself.

All he said was, "Of course you're not dying they have got treatment for cancer. Let's just wait and see what Mr Rathan has to say. I'll always be with you, we will fight this together. In a year's time we will look back on this and laugh!" But deep down he knew he was lying to her for the first time in their seven years of marriage. But sometimes you have to lie and this was one of those times. It hurt, but he had to do it.

Then Monday arrived and they were sitting in Mr Rathan's office. "Would you like a cup of tea?" he asked them.

"Please."

"How's your family... you have a daughter?"

"Yes."

"How is she?"

"Fine, thanks"

He did not say a word about her cancer for a full half an hour. Then he said, "Dr Holdworth told me he saw you both last Friday and told you about the cancer we found in the test results that I have here in front of me. Well as he told you, you have terminal cancer. I'm terribly sorry to have to tell you that it's far advanced and we can only give you treatment to slow it down and tablets to ease the pain."

"What are you saying - I'm going to die? There's nothing you can do for me?"

"Yes, I am very sorry."

"How long do I have to live?"

"Three, maybe four months." Mr Rathan was a small man, a little overweight as his waistcoat was pulling on his belly. He had a kind face - not bad looking for a man of sixty years of age. He spoke very well, he had warmth in his voice. He had to look up at John.

"Just a few more questions, you don't have to answer if you don't feel up to it."

"No I'm okay, thanks."

"Do you have any brothers or sisters?"

"No."

"Are your parents still alive?"

"Yes."

"Anyone in your family do you know of, had cancer?"

"No."

"How about you?" he asked John.

"No to the first question, yes to the second and no to the third."

"Nice to hear it."

Then it was over. "Come and see me whenever you want to," he told them.

When they got home Corre said, "Lets go away for a holiday."

"Where?"

"What about a cruise?"

"Yes I'd like that," he replied. "You know, I like that Mr Rathan, I liked the way he asked me questions, how my health was in general. What I did for a living, did I eat a lot, sleep a lot, go out too much, how my weight was, did I tire a lot and did I get headaches a lot. All these questions he asked in an easy off the cuff way - not one after the other but one question now and then. I wanted to laugh at his last question, 'Did she smoke, did you smoke, good that's three of us that don't!' It sounded funny, but he meant well."

So they booked a two week cruise in the Mediterranean. The ship they cruised on was called *Annmarie*, sister ship to *Annjoann*. It was all a rush as they got a last minute cancellation for the following Sunday. They had to pick the boat up at Southampton and had to be on board by 11'o clock as she sailed at 6'o clock that night.

It was a great holiday, and also hard work for John as not only did he have to look after Corre but his daughter as well, but it was okay.

Then it was over and they were home again. It was now five weeks from their visit to Mr Rathan and John and his family noticed the change in Corre for she stayed in most of the time, and could manage little housework. John now did most of the shopping. He was loosing weight - the pain he had to carry every day was taking its toll - seeing someone you love so much slipping away from you and knowing there is nothing you can do but just watch and pray and wait for that day that you know is not far away. How would he live without her? She was his life but soon he knew the Lord God would take her.

He looked back over the last eight years for that's how long he had known her. He remembered the time she lost her front door key when it was in her hand all the time; the day she into the wrong car by mistake - she came out of the cake shop saw this red car and got in thinking it was their car and wondering where John was. It was not until the owner of the car asked her if she was okay that she realised her mistake. Funnily, afterwards, the owner of the car became one of their close friends. And there was the time she lost her shoe on the dance floor. There were so many happy memories. The only good thing right now was his company was doing really well. His young daughter was coming up for six years. He could see what it was doing to her for like John she loved her mother so very much. They were always out together shopping, pictures, visiting her parents and many of their friends all her little secrets she shared with her mother. What would she do when her mother was not there anymore?

It was not until nearly eight weeks from the visit to Mr Rathan that Corre started to go down hill fast. Corre was sleeping most of the time. John and Corre's parents were looking after Melane'a and helping to look after Corre, taking it in turn every other day.

John's dad said, "Could they not have operated on her? Cut it out?"

"No Dad, it was too far gone. There's nothing anyone can do. She's in God's hands now. I rang Mr Rathan he said he was going to increase her drugs to help ease the pain."

"Are you sure they had the right file?"

"Dad..."

"Sorry."

"It's okay." And he put his arm round his dad.

The doctor called once a week and Mr Rathan would ring also to see how Corre was. It made John feel better she was now taking stronger drugs to help ease the pain. Before he knew it, it was ten weeks since they had seen Mr Rathan. Corre stayed in bed all the time - her eyesight was pretty bad now and half the time she did not know John or their families. He asked friends not to call, not being rude but he wanted them to remember her as she used to be. God could he hold out? Slowly he knew it was destroying him but he had to be strong for the family's sake. The doctor asked John many times if he would like to let his wife go into hospital where they would look after her. But he said, "No she is my life, what am I going to do without her?"

He would often go out into the garage and cry his heart out. How many times he cried he did not know. He told his mum, "The pain I have in my heart is so strong, it's a wonder it doesn't burst. It's not like a badly cut leg that you can see a wound and feel the pain and watch it slowly heal. This pain you can't see it, but the pain does not go away it gets worse. I would change places with Corre if I could. When I look at her asleep she is so beautiful. She is my first and only love I will never love again, I never want to. No one can ever take the place of her it is what we promised, till death do us part in this world but I'll love her while she is in the next world. Like the Vicar said last week, 'It's like your wife is going on a journey without you and when she gets to where she is going she will wait for you. It will only be a short wait then you will be together for far beyond the end of time as it says in the bible:

'For God called Mary to his house of many rooms
Saying make ready for soon you will call
Joseph to my house for his needs are of many
For you are the way, for your journey is done
His is soon to start.'"

John's mother loved her son so much that her heart cried out in pain for him. He was her only son. She knew and saw what this was doing to him and she could only be there for him.

She took his face in her hands and said, "I know son, I know." She kissed him then walked away quickly as her eyes were full of tears.

And slowly the days ticked away, it was now eleven weeks. The doctor said it was only a matter of days now as Corre slept most of the time.

It was a Thursday morning. John's mum had taken his daughter to school - most days now she stayed at John's parents house but today she had called in, she wanted to see her mum and pick up some more clothes.

He does not know why but he suddenly dropped the paper he was looking at and ran upstairs to their bedroom to Corre. She looked so peaceful and beautiful, he loved her so very much. He held her hand, she gave a kind of little squeeze to his hand and he knew he had lost her. His eyes filled with tears and he cried like a baby, calling her name over and over again. Telling her how much he loved her and everything would be okay now. He touched her cheek and talked to her, he would say, "Please come back, don't leave me I love you so much Corre. Corre!" He cried for the woman who was his life, his soulmate, his lover, mate and world. His all. For with her by his side he would take on the world. When he was down she picked him up, when things went wrong she put them right. And now his world was empty, nothing, meaningless, dead.

Then the phone rang, it was John's mum. All he said was, "Mum I've lost her!" and burst out crying again.

Within five minutes his mum was there. She rang the doctor and rang Corre's parents, then rang her husband. She was John's lifeline for the next six months, she did everything. He would just sit there in another world, would not talk or eat. His family and friends would say, "He's heading for a nervous breakdown." And if it was not for the support of his friends he would have ended up in a mental hospital. But, as they say, time heals pain but not the heart.

There were so many people at the funeral, at least three quarters of them could not get into the small chapel. It was very sad. They played her favourite tune the Beetles hit '*Let it Be*' and '*I Believe*' by Frankie Lane. So many people wanted to say goodbye to a lovely girl who died so young. She was not yet thirty years old she had everything she wanted. She loved life and life loved her but God wanted her so she had to go.

Part Two

For the next five years John devoted his life to his daughter. To make sure that she was happy he gave her almost everything she asked for. She had taken her mother's death very badly. It was a very long time before she started to be her old self again. She cried a lot, never missed going to the cemetery.

One day she asked her father if she could spend a week with her friend in the West Country. John was so happy for her that he gave her £200.00 to spend. "Thank God she is starting to be herself again," he told his mother.

"But what about you?"

"I'm alright, I've got my work."

"Why don't you just go out for a drink with your mates? It will do you good."

Over the five years so many of his friends tried to get him to go out but always he said no. But they never gave up on him. Sometimes he wanted to say yes, but felt guilty, so he always turned them down. Corre's mother and father tried, John's mother and father tried but it was not use.

"You'll be forty next year. You're still a young man. Don't throw your life away, Corre would not want that. Melane'a is now a young lady and she will soon be going out with her friends, going away on holidays. It's about time you stopped feeling sorry for yourself and got out and enjoyed yourself. We won't always be around!"

Then, whether it was his mother having a go at him or what, things changed a week later when John got a phone call from one of his best mates. He was getting married and wanted John as a witness at the local registry office on Saturday the 25th, two weeks time. Tom also worked for John's company, so it was very hard to turn down if he wanted to, as all the staff were going and it would not look very nice him being the only one not to go.

Tom said, "Bring Melane'a. It will do you both good."

So John said, "Yes."

He was living a lonely life. Melane'a was staying some nights with her best friend and some with John's parents and others with Corre's parents. He did not see a lot of her during the week or at weekends so in a way he was looking forward to going to the wedding, but it also made him feel very sad as it was at a wedding that he had met Corre nearly fourteen years before. It was Tom's second marriage, the first having failed after his wife had ran off with a bus driver and poor Tom got a lot of stick about it such as 'I bet when the bus driver said hold tight she did', or 'I bet he rang her bell a few times', or a song that was out called 'You Can Ring My Bell'. But he took it well. He said, "The marriage had been over for a long time, but I've found my dream girl in Linda."

She was a lovely girl and they made a good match.

"I'll have to get some new clothes," John announced.

But one of his mates said, "No go casual it's the thing now!"

But John went in a suit. It was the first time he had put a suit on since the funeral of Corre. It felt strange but okay.

It was a quiet wedding but there were a lot at the reception, held at a hall just along from the registry office. Most guests walked to the hall, John went with his old mate Pete. These two went back a long time, further than their school days.

At the hall John met many old mates who he had not seen in years. It was a great night and walking home he was glad he had gone. He had a few drinks and so many of his friends said, "It's great to see you out again. You've got to get out more now you've made the first move."

And it was a few days later that he got a phone call to go out for a pint for an old mates birthday.

"I'm having a drink at the Sailors Arms next Saturday, lots of the boys will be there. It will be like old times."

But John said, "No."

But his mate kept on and on and in the end to get rid of him he said, "Yes."

"I'm not going," he told himself. "I can't be bothered." But deep down he knew he wanted to go - he had the bug to go out again. He was being picked up at 8'o clock, the pub was only a few miles away. Later on he actually found himself looking forward to Saturday night.

They got to the pub around about 8.30. There were a lot of people already there as it was the best pub around for miles. You could book a meal and bed as well, if you wanted to. Lots of people came from miles around to spend a weekend there.

They had seats kept for them, so no sooner had they sat down than there were pints on the table. John already started to enjoy himself, lots of his mates turned up. It was round 10pm when three girls came in aged between twenty and thirty years old, they sat at the next table, John recognised one of the girls he saw at Tom's wedding. He did not speak to her though he saw her dancing, but took no notice of her as she was with lots of other girls. After a while Terry, whose birthday it was, started to chat up the three girls. He apparently knew the girls and had invited them to his drink up.

"What are you girls having?"

So drinks filled the tables with lots of laughing and jokes about Terry's age - he was forty-two but looked ninety-two. His mother had him when she was fifty and they would not let him live it down.

The girls bought a double round, the beer was flowing like wate. Rolls and more rolls turned up, as they were being eaten more replaced them; ham, cheese, tomato, sausage and bacon.

A friend came over to chat to John as they had not seen each other for almost two years. As one of the girls was passing a drink over it got knocked over - it went all over John's jeans.

"Sorry," she said. "I'm drunk I think!"

That made them laugh.

"No I *am* sorry!"

"It's okay these are only jeans. Iit will wash out. No harm done."

"I'll pay to have them cleaned," she told him.

"No, the old washing machine will do them okay." And so they started to chat.

"What's your name?"

"Chatlean, spelt with a C."

"Never heard that name before, or spelt like that, with a C."

"Mostly it's spelt with a K. It's an old Irish name. I've never heard of anyone else with my name!"

"What do your friends call you?"

"Chat."

"Chat. That's a funny name to be called!"

"They say I talk a lot, my best friend calls me Chatte Chat."

Then out of the blue someone called out, "Chatte, where's my drink?" That started them all laughing.

"What's your mates' names?"

"The tall one is Patsy and the other one is Jenny."

Tom, who was also there with his new bride, called over, "Watch him Chat. He's after your phone number!" Again that got them all laughing.

Then Chat said, "I know your name. It's John Canbury!"

"How do you know that?"

"I asked," she said. By this time Chat was sitting by John, "How's your jeans?"

"Okay, drying out a bit. Now what do you mean you asked?"

"Well I saw you at Tom's wedding and asked who you were. I know most of Tom's mates but have not seen you before." John had by now had a few drinks and was feeling good. It was the first time since his beloved Corre's death that he was really enjoying himself and it felt good.

It was now nearly midnight the girls said that they were going as a cab was waiting for them. "We come here every Saturday night. If you're here next week, I'll buy you a pint."

"I'll keep you to that!" he replied, and she was off. She looked back at the pub door and gave him a small wave, and a big smile.

Pete said, "You're in there mate. I've got Jenny's number - I've been trying to pull her for ages!"

"How old is she, Pete?"

"Chat? Twenty last month. You fancy her, you dirty old man!"

"Leave off, I'm nearly forty and she is twenty. I'm her age again."

"What's that got to do with it? Look at Charlie Chaplin - he was forty or fifty years older than his wife!"

All the way back to his house they ribbed him. Even after they had dropped him off at his house and were driving away they shouted back, "Cradle-snatcher. Dirty old man!"

John loved it, every minute of it and could not wait for the following Saturday night. He could not get Chat out of his mind. Had he fallen for her? This is foolish - she's probably only being friendly. After all, she had had a lot to drink that night. She must have known about Corre and felt sorry for him. He felt sick... he did not know how he felt. All he knew was that she had got to him. He knew he liked her a lot.

But on Saturday... what if she does not turn up or turns up with her boyfriend or with her mates and just says "Hello," and that's that? Luck was with him as his mates were all going to the pub that night to see a pop singer who would be there with his group. John was asked if he wanted to go and of course he said yes, but for a different reason than to see the singer. The pub was packed as usual. All had come to see a local boy who had made good and had done very well in the pop world and every now and then came back to do a gig at the pub. He did it for nothing as it was the pub landlord who put up the money for his first recording session and his first record was a smash hit.

It was 9pm and no Chat. 9.30 still no Chat. 10pm, no Chat. He kept looking at the door. By 10.30 he knew she would not show and it was then time to go home. He was sick but there was nothing he could do about it. He told his friends he wanted to walk home, so off he walked on his own, as they say 'as sick as a pig'. He could not sleep that night. Sunday he still felt sick. Monday the same, but when he got home he had three phone calls but no messages. He tried 1471 but no good, no number. Was it Chat ringing him? It got him wondering, but 10pm that night he got a phone call from a business client saying he had tried during the day to get hold of him. John was sick - he knew he had got it bad! Again he could not sleep, he was in a right mess. He went to bed, got up, watched television, back to bed and then got up again. So by the time it was time to get up he was whacked.

It was a long day. He could not get his act together. How he got through the day he didn't know, but he did, plus he got a big contract signed up that gave his company work for the next five years. So at least he got something from the day.

He didn't get home until almost 9'o clock as he had wanted to catch up on a lot of paper work and there was no need to rush home to an empty house. In a way he felt good; new contract, paperwork right up to date and the company doing great. As John opened the front door he saw a letter, just the one. It was posted from Bradly, a town eighty miles away. Who could be writing to him from there? Maybe work - he had done work for a few people over the past few years. But when he opened the letter it was from Chat. This is what was in the letter:

John

Sorry I could not see you at the pub on Saturday night. I went to see my friend's new baby and on the way back our car broke down and we had to wait for the AA to repair it. Never got it going until gone 11 so I stayed with my friend for the weekend. I'll be going up the pub Wednesday night. If you can make it, I'll see you there about 8'o clock.

Sorry I let you down,

Chatte.

PS: It's now two pints I owe you, one for the jeans and the other for not turning up Saturday. You had better turn up Wednesday as it's costing me a fortune. Only joking!

Love Chatte.

Well, if John read that letter once he read it a thousand times. He was so excited he could not sleep or eat. He was so happy that she did like him. He even took the letter up to his bedroom and read it over and over again! Roll on Wednesday - tomorrow I'll see her. He eventually did fall asleep as he was burnt out.

Again, before he went to work he read the letter four times. And at work, how many times he read the letter he himself lost count. And the only thing about the letter was that there was no address. Then it was home time, only three hours to go.

He got home and by 6.30 and was soon ready and waiting to go. Didn't want to get there too early, 8.15 would look okay. He wonder what her full name was? He knew she was twenty but did not know her date of birth. I'll ask her tonight, find out as much as I can about her.

He knew on Wednesday nights that they had dart matches - local pubs play each other and it's a good night. Well, it used to be. It had been a long time since John had had a game of darts. At one time John was a very good darts player and played for the pub and won a few cups, but that was a long time back. So he rang his mate and made out he was ringing for someone else. "Is there a game on tonight?"

"Yes there is. Are you going?"

"Don't think so."

"Come down and have a pint. Now that you are starting to come out, it'll do you good. I'll pick you up at 8'o clock okay?"

"Yes, thanks."

"Okay, it's like old times. See you at 8'o clock."

Then the phone rang again.

"It's Mick. Ray rang and said you're coming down the pub tonight?"

"Yes."

"Great. Listen, we are putting a team in tonight, want a game?"

"Don't know - I haven't played for a long time."

"Don't worry it's only a friendly."

"Okay. I'll have a go!"

After the phone call John looked for his darts, found them and got his old board out. For the next hour he practised. It felt good throwing his old darts again. "Still not bad," he said to himself.

Then it was 8'o clock and the bell rang. He was off to see Chatte and have a game of darts. His friends thought he was going to the pub to play darts, but let them think that. It got him up the pub and that was the main thing.

When they got there his mates were waiting. "John, we put you in our first team, we play Martin's Garage. We are on after the next game. Martin's Garage are a very good team and if they beat us they go on to play Claymoor Transport. So far Martin's have not lost a game. Won all the heats."

"I thought this was a friendly!" John said.

"If I told you it was a full game you might not have wanted to play!" John shook his head. "If they get beaten tonight we have a good chance of getting through to the next round."

The pub was starting to fill up, most of the people had

come to see the dart matches. "If we could beat them it would be one up on them. With you in our team we've got a good chance."

"Don't bank on it, I have not played for a long time." All the time John was talking, he was looking for Chatte.

Then he saw her. God she was beautiful. She saw him, waved and had a big smile for him as she came over. "Hello!"

"Hello. Car okay now?"

"Yes, just about."

"Want a drink?"

"Please. Let's find a seat." He got the drinks and they found a seat and they talked and talked, laughed a lot, and he loved every second of it.

Then it was his team's turn to play. As he got up to go, Chatte leant over and kissed him on the cheek. "Good luck."

"Thank you."

It was a good game and it only took him a few throws to throw like he used to. After each throw he would look at Chatte. She would smile at him and it made him feel good. He played like a champion. All he needed was double seven for the game. Double seven it was! What a noise; shouting, banging, laughing and the pub went mad. He was so happy. Deep down he hated Martin's Garage for they were all big heads and to see them get beaten made his day and night. Also Mick was a very close friend of his. He was there all the way through the funeral and always calling round and ringing him to make sure John and his daughter were alright. So it was very special for him to win.

What a night! Drinks flowed like water, Chatte went mad hugging and kissing him. She laughed and cried and squeezed his hand. She was so happy for John and deep down she knew she was falling in love with him. And something, she did not know what, told her he was in love with her. The way he kept looking at her, wanted her by his side, held her hand. They carried him round the pub and what a noise. They were through to the next round and with John in the team they could go all the way. It was talk of the week, even if you don't play darts or like it, it still made you feel good, gave you a funny feeling. "Tonight's win," one of John's friends said, "is better than my team winning the FA cup!"

For many, many people hated Martin's Garage darts team, not because they won almost every game but because they were so big headed. One player had said, "We are the best we only play you for practise!" So when they got beaten by John's dart team it was a double victory for the supporters. They made John captain and he loved it. But deep, deep down he couldn't help feeling guilty for laughing, being happy and out drinking and being with another woman, while his first love, his wife, the mother of his child lay dead not more than four miles away for the last eight years. She had not been much older than Chatte when she died.

After it was all over and it was time to go home John and Chatte walked back to his home arm in arm, stopping, kissing non-stop talking by Chatte. To John it was music to his ears. It took over an hour to get home. So time did not matter. What did matter? John was with Chatte because she wanted to be with him and that was all that he wanted out of this world that night. And dare he wish have many, many more nights with her?

At John's house Chatte made some toast and coffee and they sat talking. Chatte said, "You would have been in big trouble if you had not asked me back for coffee!"

"Oh, I'm glad I did then." They laughed, it was good to laugh again. He was so happy that he felt like a schoolboy.

"I knew you were good at darts. I know all about you."

"Who told you?"

"None of your business!" she laughed.

They got on so well that first night it was as if they had been courting for months. She stayed the night. John made her breakfast the next morning and they spent the day together. Chatte had a laugh that made you laugh and John loved to listen to it. It was a laugh that was innocent and fresh, honest and true and also funny. He would laugh just by listening to her laugh and she would punch him and say, "I hate you," and again they would both laugh. He would kiss her and hug her. God was he happy.

They popped up the pub for a pint and to have lunch and the drinks were on the pub. It was gone 3'o clock by the time they got back to John's house. "I bet they're wondering where I got to. I was supposed to go into work today, but I'm glad you told me not to." And again she started to laugh. So it to be the start of a beautiful love affair. At 10'o clock that night he took her home and they kissed good night.

"God she's beautiful!" he said as he watched her walk up to her door. She waved and then went in.

During the next months they were together everyday. John's friends and family were happy to see him out again, laughing and back to his old self. They went on to win the darts championships inter-pub cup and again winning on the last dart, thrown by John.

It was about two months since John and Chatte had been going out, when his mum and dad called round to see him.

"You know son, with all the work you've got, and now you're courting Chatte, we think it would be better if Melan'a came and lived with us. She's growing up so fast and needs a lot of attention and love. We're not saying that you don't give her these things, but she needs much more that you are giving her. You know lots of nights you don't get home until late and she spends most of her life with us now anyway."

"You know Mum," John replied, "it's been playing on my mind too. Have you spoken to Melan'a. I want her to be happy."

"No, we wanted to speak to you first."

He knew his mum and dad were completely right.

"If you both pop round tonight then, we can talk to her."

But John need not have worried. Melan'a adored her grandparents, and with all the things they offered her, how could she refuse! At her grandparents' house she had her own bedroom, her own television and friends could come round whenever and even stay overnight. Plus two sets of pocket money from both her father and her grandparents! But the deciding factor was that she loved her Nan and Grandad very much. Her dad was very busy at work and now with Chatte in his life, she spent most of her time at her grandparents' anyway. She was happy there.

John said he would see her as often as he could in the week and at weekends. He promised to ring her every day and never once let her down. Although he was sad to see her go, he knew it was for the best and the right thing to do for Melan'a.

John and Chatte soon went away on holiday. They just could not get enough of each other. When apart, he used to ring her four times a day just to hear her voice. He was so in love with her and she with him. When they were together the world could have split in half and they would not have known. They lived for each other. Nothing mattered in his world as long as they were together. What used to go through his mind was that he loved his wife so much he did not think a man could love another woman stronger. To him his wife was his life, but here he was madly in love again. This love was different. He never felt like this with his first wife. For one, he could not get her out of his mind. Two, when he was not with her he was unhappy, longed to see her be with her. Three, he worried like mad if she was late ringing him or meeting him. Some days she was not well and he would panic until she was okay again. He would cook, wash, do the housework, shopping, anything she wanted done and he loved every minute of it. True, he had helped his wife and had done everything that he was doing for Chatte, but it was completely different. He could not explain it, all he knew was he was in love, very much in love and he wanted it to stay that way forever.

He tried not to put one against the other, like everyone in this world we all have our faults, he was at the top of the list for faults and he knew it. Chatte loved everything his wife had loved, going out, staying in, watching television, parties, shows, having friends round, all the things lovers do. But this love, again he would say it, was so powerful, so strong and deep and so true. There was so much love between them it was as if God had given them all the love that was in the world, as they were as one with each other, there was nothing, nothing, life was nothing, as he felt for her so she felt for him.

It was as if she was his shadow. While she was his shadow, life was the sun, moon, music, laughter and again the same was for her. Without the shadow life was meaningless. The day was dead, the night empty, so empty that if the sun shone on him it was cold, if it was cold he did not feel it. He got very aggravated very quickly, did not listen if some one was talking to him all he could do was think about her all the time. Did she love him? But he knew she loved him. Was there someone else? But he knew there was no one else. Was he jealous and was it taking hold of him? No. At a party she would chat to all the fellows, it did not upset him. He was scared of losing her but why should he lose her? Yet it was always at the back of his mind.

These same things went through Chatte's mind day in, day out and like John she was scared of losing him. She used to say, "God's been good to me. Look what I've found, everything a woman could ever want. Thank you, Lord. This gift from God, was it a gift? Is love a gift? You tell me" To Chatte God had given them the most precious gift in life. Love. Real, deep, powerful love. It was love, love that God had given to two people that would never bend, crack, split, break or part - but most of all would never end. Only death could do that. And death may end their living lives but not their love for each other.

As you looked at them the love between them almost spoke out. It was so beautiful to see. The world only dreams of having love like theirs. But only a few ever get it and then some lose it very quickly. Some keep it for life and some don't realise what they've got. The Lord God watches, looks down and smiles, for he is happy. To him they are his children. When children are happy the troubles of the world are left far behind, the Lord God gave this world his love and many gave their love back. Without love in this world it is dead. As the saying goes:

It is better to have loved and lost,
Than to never have loved at all.

It was teatime, Friday afternoon. Chatte was at work she had just made a cup of tea and was carrying it on a tray to the tea room when she dropped it. It just fell out of her hands. That night when she got back to John's house she had a bad headache. She lay down and fell asleep. John was working until 10'o clock so by the time he got home she was okay again. So she never said anything to him. Why should she?

It was almost a month later that she started to get a lot of pins and needles in her hands and some days felt dizzy and sick. Was she going to have a baby? But the home test told her no.

They went on a week's holiday and everything was fine. But a few days after their holiday she felt unwell so stayed in bed for a few days. John had time off work. Chatte made a cup of tea but as she walked back into the bedroom she dropped it. It was as if her hands by themselves had let the cup go. The headaches had got more frequent, she felt sick most days. Almost now once a week would drop something. It was now starting to worry her. She still had not said a word to John but she decided to go and see the doctor. She told John she was going to drop some paperwork off. It worked well as he had some people coming round to look at his work so he could not go with her.

Chatte told the doctor everything.

"I think I'll send you for some tests."

"Can you let me know the dates for them as I don't want my boyfriend to know. He's a worrier."

"I'll leave the letter in reception for you to collect. Say for Friday, is that okay?"

"Yes."

"Good. I'll give you a check over now and ask a few questions." So for the next half an hour the doctor asked this and that, pressed this and touched that.

After he had finished she asked, "What do you think is wrong?"

"It looks to me as if you've burnt yourself out. Get out of the fast lane for a while. You can't burn the candle at both ends. Take these twice a day, it's a pick up. Once I get the results from the tests you go for, I'll call you in to see me. It takes about six weeks at the moment they are very short staffed at the hospital because of this flu that's sweeping the country."

And that was that. Chatte felt better. It was not serious. She decided not to say anything to John. So she dropped the paperwork off and went home to him. They had been living together now for a few months and he loved it. They were going to sell the house and buy another one. A fresh start, so to speak, new home new life and they hoped to have a baby of their own one day. John's company had made and was making him a lot of money as he had bought the company outright but the same people worked for him. So she could leave her job if and when she fell for a baby, without worrying over money.

So life for both of them was looking really good. Just got to get this dizziness and headaches out of the way, thought

Chatte. They were both in no rush to get married, but if she was to fall for a baby they would get married before it was born. So, without telling each other, they both hoped for a baby. But they loved each other and were together, that was the main thing.

During the six week wait for the results Chatte dropped more things and got pins and needles, dizziness, headaches and felt sick, but all the time she never told John. As luck would have it, if you call it luck, he was never around when they occurred. She also started to lose weight - she told John she wanted to lose a few pounds and he was happy with that. But one morning on her day off she went to get out of bed and she lost her balance completely and fell down. She was so dizzy that she did not know where she was for the moment and did not have the strength to get up. She just lay on the floor for nearly an hour. When she did try to get up it was very difficult as she felt so tired and weak. She had also lost her sight for a little while. She lay on the bed and fell asleep.

The next thing she knew it was three in the afternoon, John would be home in a few hours. She had not done a thing in the house or anything else she had planned. It was a bad day for Chatte. John usually got home around 7'o clock but he rang to say he had a lot of work on and wanted to clear it all up today. Chatte was glad in a way. She had a shower, got dressed and felt not too bad and made a light meal for John. He never noticed anything wrong with her as she was good at covering up her illness.

A week later she got a phone call asking her to go up the hospital to see them. So on Monday she got up as usual and waited until John left. She told him she had a day's holiday left at work, and she was taking it today.

She got to the hospital at 11.20am and went straight to see Mr Wanton.

"I'm very sorry to have to tell you that I have the results of your tests and its bad news," he said. "You have cancer and it's malignant. We cannot do anything for you. I'm terribly sorry."

"How long do I have to live?" she eventually asked. Did he know she thought to herself. I've got to find out sooner or later.

"The most I can say is three months."

"Oh God no!" She broke down and cried her eyes out.

Mr Wanton got her a cup of tea and for the next hour had a long talk with her, telling her what to expect in that time.

How she got home she never knew. When she got there she sat on the bed in a daydream for most of the day. "What am I to do? I cannot tell John, he's been through it once it would not be fair!" She was too tired to think so she lay back on the bed and fell asleep.

She woke at 3.30 the phone had woken her up it was John. "Hello Chatte, how did your day go? Buy lots of clothes?"

"No, I didn't see anything I liked."

"What no clothes, you must be ill! I'll take you up town Saturday. You're bound to see something you like. Are you okay?"

"Yes, fine."

"Great. Fine. See you five to half past, okay? Bye."

"Bye," and she put the phone down.

So the next hour she sat and worked out what she was going to do. She knew that the following week he had to go to a meeting to sign a contract for three years giving the company more work. He had to go up north and would be away at least three days, so she set her plans for those days he was away. First she rang her best friend asking if she could go and stay with her. Of course she could. Second, she had to hand in her notice in work. Third, pick out a time to leave over the three days John was away. The third day was best, for John would ring morning and evening to make sure she was okay.

"I'll tell him not to ring on the morning of the third day," she said to herself. "Say I will be out."

She could get all her clothes into her friend's car. Jenny lived one hundred and sixty-four miles away. John knew Jenny, but not where she lived. So when he got home late he would find her gone.

So she acted as normal as possible and on the morning he was going up north she kind of told him in fun, "Don't ring at 11'o clock at night like you usually do. A girl's got to get her beauty sleep. Nor at six in the morning because you can't sleep!" With lots of hugging and kissing and tears she said goodbye to the man she loved so much. She would always love him till the day she died. It hurt her a lot to think of that. After he had gone she lay on the bed and cried her eyes out for a long, long time. She hated everybody, even the world. Only her John she loved. She wanted to give him lots of babies. Love him for a thousand years. Just to think of him made her happy. And to think of the many times he made her laugh. The time it took him to do up his shoelaces when he had hurt his thumb - over fifteen minutes and he would not give up! And what made it worse was the laces were very short and he found them hard to hold. Oh there were so many happy times they had together now it was all gone. All she had to look forward to was dying. She hated God. "Why did you do this to us, has he not suffered enough? Now he's got to go through it all again. Well, he won't. I won't let you do that to my John."

She had gone over and over and over the letter she had written to him. It was lies from beginning to end. She hated herself for writing it, but it was for his sake. She could not bear to let him know the truth.d "He must never know. After a while he will hate me and find someone else. I just pray I'm strong enough to hold out for the next three months!"

This is the letter she wrote to him:

John,

For a long time now I've had mixed feelings for you. At one time I thought I was in love with you but I know now it was a crush or whatever you might like to call it. To tell you the truth John I don't love you and I don't want to live with you anymore. I could never marry you either. You're a nice man but not for me, I want to go out with my friends, to party, holidays, be free again - but I can't because I'm tied down. I hate this house and everything in it. I'm taking all the things that belong to me. I've left your ring - thanks, but no thanks. Don't try to find me because you will only be wasting your time. Just stay out of my life. We had fun, now it's over, so keep away from me. Any mail for me give or send it to my mother. I'm sorry to say you loved me but I never loved you.

Goodbye

Chatte.

It was the most painful letter she had ever had to write. Thank God it would be the one and only. Many times she wanted to rip it up but she had to be strong for them both. Then the phone rang, it was Jenny. "Alright to come round?"

"Yes, he's gone."

About twenty minutes later she was knocking on the front door. Chatte showed her the letter to John and they both cried. Jenny gave her lots of hugs. "It will be alright. Don't worry, I'll always be with you."

"Thank you, you are a good friend."

"Am I not your best friend?"

"Yes," and they both laughed.

For the next two days they packed all her clothes. Jenny had an estate car so everything of hers went into the car with ease.

Now it was the third day. Chatte had spoken to John the night before, so no more phone calls it was time to go. She left the house keys, letter and money John had given her on the table. He would see the letter as soon as he went into the front room to look for her. She took one last look around. She had been so happy living there, had so many happy memories. She closed the door quietly, she and Jenny drove away slowly. She did not look back for there were tears in her eyes. They never spoke a lot on the way back to Jenny's. By the time Jenny got to her home Chatte had fallen asleep.

John got home around about 8'o clock that night. There had been a bad accident and it had cost him another two hours on his journey. Strange, he thought as he pulled up outside the house, no lights on. It worried him he opened the front door, put the light on and called out, "Chatte! Chatte, I'm home!" No answer. He went into the kitchen, put the light on then ran upstairs to the bedroom. No Chatte. He ran downstairs into the front room then he saw the letter, keys and money. He picked up the keys, put them down, picked up Chatte's letter sat down and read it.

He was sick inside. Could not believe his eyes. Tears came so quickly that he could not read the letter. He read it over and over. He was just dumbstruck, dead inside. He read it again and again. He rang her mother, no answer. He rang the friend she worked with and she told John that she had left the post office, given her notice in last week. No idea where she is.

He rang his parents. No, they had not seen her for over a week.

"We will come over?"

"No. I'll see you tomorrow."

He ran off to the bedroom again. All her clothes were gone, nothing of her left. All gone. He rang all her friends and all said the same. They had not seen her. Too late to ring the doctor. Was she ill? Did she have money problems? Had she gone off with another man? No, it was none of those. So what was it?

He could not sleep that night, was up and down kept going to the window every time he heard a car go by. It was driving him mad. He was a physical wreck with worry. He loved her so much. The pain was terrible, but what could he do? How could he find her? Where to start? But she said don't try to find her, she does not love him.

"Help me, God. Please help me to find her. But where do I start?"

On the way to her friend's home Chatte had the radio on and of all the records to play they played their song, '*I'll always Love You*' by Jerry Cane, a country and western singer - not a big star but he had a good voice. Hearing the song sent her into a very low mood and she started crying again. She so much wanted to turn back. She was missing John already. She had not seen him for three days. But she loved him so much she had to do what she was doing for his sake.

Then they were at her friend's home. Jenny had got her room ready and told her, "I'll bring everything in then I'll go and make us a cup of tea."

Chatte looked so ill. Her eyes were very puffed up, her face pale and lost. Jenny wanted to hug her and cry with her but she knew she had to be strong for her friend would soon die. Like Chatte she asked, "Why Lord, did you do it? Why? You can see she's only a baby. She's done nothing wrong. Her only sin was to fall in love with a lovely fellow. Two people in love and you have to break them up! Why?" All this went through her mind and lots more. God she wanted to scream, shout, cry herself.

They say God does not care or listen. If he did why is there so much suffering in the world and he does nothing about it? But in Chatte's case he did listen and he did care and help her. One, Jenny was her best friend, two - Jenny was not working, did not have to as she had been left some money. Not a lot but enough to stay our of work for the next three months to look after Chatte. Three - Jenny was a nurse of seven years and part of her job was to look after cancer patients who were too ill to stay at home and to put it simply were just waiting to die. Death is not a nice thing, Jenny had seen many people, young and old, come into the hospital and die. So God had helped, Jenny being a best friend and nurse. Why he was going to take Chatte

out of this world only he knows. He had given Chatte the chance
to find real love, good strong love, warm happy love, real love
not just a five minute wonder. There are many in this world
who never find love real love as the old saying goes:

If you find true love be true to you love.

So let's move on with our story and you will see what God
can do. But first don't try to work out why God did this. Do
not do that, because throughout time no one, and I mean no
one, has found the answer.

The next day Chatte cried her little heart out. Did not sleep,
could not eat. Jenny was with her all the time; she made a bed
up in the same room as Chatte so she was always near her if she
wanted something during the night.

John also could not sleep or eat. Daytime could not come
quick enough for him. He had to find her and nothing would
stop him. He would say to her, "Tell me to my face that you
don't love me, have never loved me!" Over and over he would
work out what to say to her and every time it was different.

From 8'o clock onwards he was on the phone to everyone
who knew her. He rang and rang the post office, he made over
twenty-five phone calls and nothing! He rang his company and
told them he would not be in till the following Monday. By the
end of the day he was a wrecked man and was still no closer to
finding her than he was at 8'o clock that morning.

Before he knew it, it was nearly a week since she had left
him. In that week Chatte had gone downhill very fast. She was
getting a lot of blurred vision, dizzy spells and was now in bed
a lot of the time. Jenny never left her side. She did a lot of
crying, sometimes in the night she would call out for John. It
hurt Jenny a great deal to see her best friend like this and she
wanted to ring John and tell him where Chatte was and how ill
she was and that she really did love him very much. But she held
back.

It was now over a month since she had left John. He had

lost a lot of weight, looked ill and still could not sleep very well. He did not eat too much and it did not matter what food his mother put in front of him he pushed it away.

Jenny knew by different signs that the way Chatte was her time was running short, very short. "I've got to ring John," she told her mother, "I'm loosing her fast."

Jenny's mother said, "Do it now, don't wait or think about it."

"But it's 11'o clock at night..."

"Jenny ring him now!" her mother said. "Ring John now." So she did. He answered the phone almost as soon as it rang,

"John this is Jenny, Chatte's friend."

"Oh, hello Jenny."

"I've got Chatte with me at my house. She's dying, John. Can you get to my place?"

"Yes, I'm on the way!" So Jenny gave directions to her home. Five minutes later he was on his way to Chatte. All the way to her he cried. At last he was there.

Jenny took him straight to see her she was fast asleep. He looked at her. God how he loved her. He sat on the bed and took her hand and kissed it and cried like a baby. Jenny went out and closed the door. He cried uncontrollably and kept saying, "Please don't leave me, I love you. Please don't leave me, I'm no good without you. I love you. Please don't leave me, I'll look after you. I promise. Please, please." And the more he spoke to her the more he cried.

About half past three Jenny knocked and came in, "John I've made something to eat and want to talk to you." It was hard to leave her but Jenny got him out of the bedroom and she told him everything, missing out nothing. John never said a word just sat there and listened to her.

"How long do you think she has got?" he asked.

"A month, at the very most."

"Oh God! What am I going to do without her? I love her

so much. She is my life. Is there no cure?"

"No John. There's nothing anybody can do for her. It's God's will!"

So for the rest of the night they sat and talked.

"Can I take her out in the car?"

"Yes, but she gets very tired very quickly. She's not the same girl you last saw. She's very ill, John. Her memory is going, her sight, her coordination is almost gone. But saying that you can talk to her. There's still lots she can do."

It was about six in the morning that Jenny said to him, "Why don't you try and get some sleep? She won't wake up until about 10'o clock. I'll call you as soon as she wakes."

"I don't think I'll be able to sleep."

"Try."

John went into the front room and lay down on the settee and closed his eyes and fell asleep. Jenny woke him up at 11'o clock

"Chatte is sitting up in bed. She does not know you are here. Go in and see her."

As he opened the door Chatte looked over. It was a picture that John said afterwards he would never forget. For from a sad lonely pale-faced young girl that once was so pretty changed in seconds. Her eyes came alive. The same smile was so beautiful from a lonely sad young girl. She was John's very beautiful woman who he loved more than life. She was his Chatte.

"John!" she cried out on seeing him. He ran to her. Her arms open, she hung on to him as if her life depended on it. As weak as she was her grip was tight, she kissed him many times laughing, crying at the same time, saying over and over again, "I love you, I love you, I love you. I'm sorry. I do love you. Don't leave me please."

"Now that I've found you, I'll never leave you!"

Jenny looked in, smiled with tears in her eyes and closed the door, sat in the armchair and fell asleep.

What they talked about or what happened in that room we will never know but whatever happened it gave Chatte great happiness. The colour came back into her face. She seemed to have more strength in her body and she laughed at whatever John was saying.

Jenny told John he could stay until the end. He had now been at Jenny's seventeen days. He had taken Chatte out about eight times but each time it was getting harder for her. But she loved going out, just for a ride. Most of the time she was asleep, but John was happy just to have her by his side. To him that was all that mattered.

He asked Chatte why she had left him. "I love you very much," she told him. "I know of the pain you went through with your wife I could not let you go through that all over again. It was the only way I could save you that terrible pain again. Why should you go through it twice? Once was bad enough. But it was the hardest decision I've ever had to make. Please believe me, it was for you John."

"Shush," he said as he touched her lips with his finger. "It's okay. We are together now. But thank you. If I could change places with you now I would."

This time she touched his lips and said, "Kiss me."

Later that day he said to Jenny, "One morning Chatte wants me to take her down the coast. She wants to look at the sea. What do you think? Is it possible or what? Whatever you say I'll do."

"Well, you know it's only a very little time that she's got left. I don't think she's got the strength to walk or do anything."

"I'll carry her to the car. We can park so she can look out to sea."

"That will be the only way you can take her out."

So he told Chatte that they were going down the coast, but she was not well at all that week and she stayed in bed. But on the Sunday she said in a soft voice, "Please take me down to the sea, I want to smell it, please!" So he got her dressed. She wanted to put on the dress she had worn the first time he had taken her out.

"I want to go at night time." So at 8'o clock he set off to the coast. It was a very hot night, it was in the middle of July. They got to the coast at around 9.15. Luck was with them, they parked right on the sea front. But her eyesight was not very good.

"I love the smell of the sea air," she told him.

Her voice was so quiet that he leant over and kissed her. "I know I remember," and he laughed.

They sat there for a very long, long time not saying a word he held her hand. It looked to him like she was asleep but then a dog started barking and she very slowly looked to where the barking came from. On the beach two men were fishing the tide was in. John sat and watched them, telling Chatte about them. It was one of the things John loved himself as a boy. He was always fishing, fishing and darts. Fishing as a boy, darts as a man.

"It must be ten years since I last went fishing, just don't seem to get the time anymore with a company to run." It looked like it was going to rain they could hear thunder in the distance and lightning far out to sea.

Chatte gave a small squeeze on his hand and said, "Why don't you go and watch the fishing for a while? I'll be okay it will do you good."

"No. I'll stay here with you," he said.

"Okay," she joked, "I'll let you go for five minutes, but only five okay?" They both laughed.

"Are you sure you will be okay?"

"Of course I'll be okay. I've got you haven't I?"

"You know you have forever."

"Kiss me. then go!" As he got out of the car she said, "John I love you."

"I love you!" He blew a kiss to her and walked over to the fishermen on the beach. Every now and then he would look back at the car. He stayed on the beach for about ten minutes. He walked slowly back to the car, got in and looked at Chatte. Was she asleep?

"Oh God, no! Please no!" While he was on the beach she had died in her sleep. A sleep that only God can wake you from. He hugged her and cried, "No, no please don't go Chatte, please don't go I love you so much. Please God don't take her from me please. Chatte please wake up. Please don't leave me. Oh God what am I going to do?"

But there was nothing he could do. He drove slowly to the hospital that was only a mile away. He told them all about her illness. By now it had started to rain very heavily. It was 4.30 in the morning when he came out of the hospital. The wind had picked up and it was now raining very, very heavily. He had parked his car across the road. Head down against the wind and rain no coat on only a t-shirt and jeans. In seconds he was soaked through. He never saw the bus and the bus never saw him...

Clown Of Tears

Let's go back to 1890, to a small town called Trapani, in Sicily, where Cilo Cakari was born on May 12th. His mother was in her late forties when she had him and she always maintained her son was 'an accident'. But it is also said her marriage was not too good as her husband Janor was seeing another woman and the only way to keep her husband was to fall for another baby. So here we have Cilo Cakari. He was a small baby and the doctors said he would be lucky if he survived, as he had only just made it into this world.

Marqua was the name of the woman Cilo's father was seeing but as soon as he heard about his wife having a baby he stopped seeing her. He had been married twenty-two years and had one daughter, twelve-year-old Caddeka, but he so much wanted for a son. But it never happened until the 12th May 1890.

Marqua was a very beautiful woman who could have any man she wanted. She had never married and was also very strange as she had mystic powers. In England you might call her a witch. Those who crossed her paid a heavy price. She loved Janor and wanted him for her own. She blamed Cilo for her losing Janor. She said, "If Cilo had not been born then Janor would be mine!" He and his mother would pay a heavy price.

Three months later Cilo's mother died and the doctors at that time could not work out why she died, as she was a healthy woman. She just said, "I don't feel well" lay down on her bed and died. But the strange thing was, as she lay dead on the bed with the doctor looking down at her, tears started to run down her cheeks. Seeing the tears the doctor said, "She must still be alive." But on closer examination it was obvious that she was dead. No one in the room at that time could give answers to why tears started to run down her face. Afterwards the doctor asked other doctors, but none came up with a good or right answer. Cilo was taken in by Janor's sister and in the first five years of his life, many a time they thought they were going to lose him. He was not a healthy strong boy, small for his age and well under weight.

Cilo was loved very much by his father and his sister's family they brought him up as one of their own. They had three boys and two girls and were a very close and happy family. Not a lot is known about Cilo until he got to the age of ten. At ten he was a good-looking boy and all the girls chased after him. He was slim and grew to five foot three inches. The most he ever weighed was around eight stone.

There was a small circus was in their village and of course everybody wanted to go. In those days if you did not have the money to go and see the show you could barter with the ring master with things such as potatoes, fruit, pots, pans, clothing or do repairs to the travelling wagons, even help the circus people. It was the same circus that came twice a year and almost the whole village went. The only ones who did not go were those who chose not to.

The circus had horses, bears, one tiger, a funny looking very large brown pig, rope walkers, four very small white ponies, three monkeys, two snakes and of course clowns – four clowns who all through the show got in the way of the acts going on. They got told off many times by the ringmaster and of course made the villagers laugh many times throughout the show. Cilo could not take his eyes off them, with their funny painted faces, clothes of many bright colours and the things they got up to. He laughed and jumped up and down. He laughed when they threw water over his friend and laughed even more when they threw water over him. But the most treasured moment of the whole show was when the clown, Meme, picked him out of his seat and took him into the middle of the ring on his shoulders and all the other clowns started to squirt water at him. Cilo loved every minute of it.

Then it was over he was back in his seat but that was a start of a new world he entered and stayed in for eighty years. Cilo held the record for being the longest and oldest still performing clown in the world, when at the age of ninety he died. But we have gone too far forward. Let's stay at Cilo being ten and the circus. It usually stayed in the village for four days - only then off they would go again to another village. In those days Cilo would hang around the circus doing little jobs, running errands and messages. As long as he was with the circus people he was very happy. He asked many times if he could move on with them but they always said, "No you're too young. You've got to be strong but most of all you've got to stay at school. And what would your auntie say if you came with us? She would be very unhappy!"

He asked his aunt and his father over and over, but the answer was always no. The circus people would say, "If your father says yes then you can come with us."

But his father would always say, "If the circus people say yes then you can go!" So between the circus people and his father he had no chance. But when the circus left the village so did Cilo and on one knew he had left. Cilo had worked out a plan. He asked his father if he could stay with Mario Cancee and his family for a few weeks. He knew his father would let him, so for two weeks he had plenty of time to travel with the circus before his father found out that he had not gone and stayed with Mario's family. He would hide in one of the caravans for a few days. He knew what he wanted to do with his life starting now and that was he wanted to be a clown. Not just any old clown but the best in the world. He wanted to be rich, famous and the best there ever was and the best there will ever be. He wanted this so badly that he would give up everything to be the best clown in the world. He also believed that his mother died having him so he wanted to be the best not only for himself but for his mother too. Even at ten years of age he had mapped out his own life and no one would cheat him of his destiny.

For Cilo was this the start of a new life. There was nothing in his village to do except work the fields, work on the new road being built into the village, build new cottages - all of which Cilo had no desire to do now or in the future. All he wanted to be was a clown and a clown he would one day be. If his father took him back he would run off again and again until he was old enough to leave home.

It was two days later that Cilo was caught stealing bread late at night by the ringmaster himself and he was not very happy with Cilo. He called Cara, the fortune-teller in to look after Cilo. The boy told Von Gattor the ringmaster why he had run away, but Von Gattor said he had to go back as he would get the circus into a lot of trouble for keeping a ten year old boy. No matter how he pleaded the ringmaster would not give way.

"You're going back, that's the end of it. It will take us another day to get to our next village and there I will send a message to your father. Liko Zarika the tinker and his family will be at Quaka, our next village, you can go back with them. You can earn your keep while you are with us working with the Zolly brothers and their horses."

But Cilo had his own plans of the work he wanted to do, so he went to Comeko the circus's top clown and told him he was to work with him. Cilo knew he had two weeks before his father found out he was missing or only a week if he was taken back to his village by Liko Zarika and his family. Things were not looking good for Cilo.

When Cara saw him she loved him right away. To Cara, Cilo was the boy she never had but always wante. Cara was thirty years old. Never married, many lovers but never a bride. All she knew was the circus she was born into. Her mother was known as Zathana the Queen of the fortune-tellers. She never knew her father. Cara was five foot, plump, happy, warm and a loving woman, always ready to help anybody if she could. She would always listen to people's troubles and help if she could, and many times she did. She would always be looking after some circus people's children, she just loved children so much. When she was given Cilo to look after, in one way her life was complete.

It happened that she was to look after Cilo for the rest of her life. She once said, "God was good to me, he never gave me a son of my own but he gave me Cilo. He is my son, my life, my happiness for without him I know I would die. I love him so much."

Cilo never wanted for anything. He loved Cara with all his young blood and heart. He called her Mother Cara. All through their lives together he would ask her advice on everything. They had no secrets from one another, even about girlfriends as he got older. It was God's wish Cara dreamt Cilo happiness that made it perfect in every way.

When they got to Quaka, Liko Zarika was not there. He had only stayed one day and moved on. He did not say where he was going so there was no one going back to Cilo's village. "I'll send a message to your father. In the meantime you can stay with us." the ringmaster said. To Cara he added, "He is your responsibility. Look after him and keep him out of my way and find him a job."

Cara and Cilo laughed and hugged one another for in one day their fate was sealed for life. And what a life! They gave each other so much love and happiness for the next forty-seven years.

When, ten days later, Janor got the message of Cilo running off with the circus he did not know what to do. He had no idea he had run off and he had very little money to go and bring him back. He also he did not know where the circus was. In the message it said, "*As soon as I can I'll get him back to you. Do not worry I will make sure that he is looked after, fed and well clothed.* The ringmaster Von Gattor."

Von Gattor was a German and his father once owned a circus in Germany many years back called Von Gattor's Flying Circus. Janor went to Marqua to see if he could borrow money to go and get his son but she said, "Marry me and I'll give you all the money you want."

But he replied, "No. I do not love you and do not want to marry you!"

"You fool!" she screamed at him. "You will pay for that insult" And he did. A few weeks later Janor was staying with his sister and announced, "I don't feel well, I think I'll lie down for a while." But a few hours later when his sister went to see how he was he was dead. She called the doctor but he did not know what Janor had died of. As his sister, her husband and the doctor were looking at him laying on the bed, tears started to roll down his cheeks. His sister cried out, "Look he is still alive!"

But then the doctor looked at him and said, "No he is dead. The tears are just like his wife's. I don't know what to make of it, it is too much for me."

Many villagers believed it was the evil work of Marqua for being turned down by Janor. Was Marqua trying to make life even worse - causing more pain and suffering by making the dead cry?

But did something in Marqua's evil go wrong? For they say to curse evil on the good is to curse evil on your soul. Two months after Janor's death she stabbed her new lover Mario after he told her he was leaving her for another woman. He died trying to get out of her bed with a knife in his back. She hung herself a few days later in the local police station that was once a horse stable . She used a long horse whip hung from a beam running across the stable ceiling.

Cilo did not know of his father's death for almost a year. Neither did he know of that of Marqua or Mario who was known to Cilo as he had often played with Mario's twins.

So Cilo went and started work for Comeko, filling the buckets of water, getting ladders, boxes, skipping ropes, everything that the clowns used in their show. Everybody loved Cilo for he would do anything to help. Comeko and his clowns loved him and would show him lots of tricks. How to feel sad, look sad, feel happy, look happy, be silly and do everything to get the people to laugh at him but also to love him. Cilo worked long hours and after his work would just sit and watch the clowns rehearse, day in and day out. He never got tired. He would laugh, jump up and down, shouting out. He lived just for the clowns and slowly he got to know every trick.

He knew the act inside and out. Sometimes they would let him do a trick in the act, dress him up and paint his face and then they would call him into the ring and throw buckets of water over him. He then had to walk slowly off looking back with a sad lonely face. The crowd would go silent and just watch. One lady jumped into the ring and started to hit Comeko with her potato bag. The crowd loved it and when Comeko called Cilo back into the ring the people went mad shouting and clapping, banging the wooden seats and whistling. After many bows finally they let him go. It was then that Comeko knew Cilo was something special and all the circus people that day realised they had a star, a very special star.

Then luck really did step in for Clio. Micro broke his leg very badly and had to leave the circus for a while so Cilo was given a trial run to see if he was up to it before they sent for another clown to make up the four-man team. At the end of their act again buckets of water were thrown over Clio, and then he was sent off. The crowd got very angry and Comeko called Cilo back into the ring. He took bows and he had his own gimmick; he would do one of his own tricks that he had made up. The crowd loved it and shouted, "More, more!" And then he would do another trick, wave then run off. He was only eleven years old.

Throughout the land his name spread like wildfire and every night the shows were packed out. Many people went twice just to see Cilo's act. The women loved him and the men wanted him for their son. He got lots of clothes, toys, presents and even money and all the time Cara watched him, protected him and kept his feet on the ground. After every show he would look for her, as she would stand in the same place every night. He would look over to her, wave, throw kisses to her and run out of the ring straight to her. He would hug her tight, she would kiss him then go back to their caravan feed him and then tuck him up in bed. She would then wash and mend his clothes for the next show. He always asked her what she thought and whatever she said he would do and his act got better and better.

She was now known as Mother Cara by all the circus people. She still did her fortune telling but found it hard to put the time in as she was always doing something for Cilo. But with the money Cilo was bringing into the circus, the ringmaster said she could spend all her time looking after Cilo plus he would give her a wage. Cilo did not get paid but the money thrown into the ring was enough money to feed him and Cara, so they both lived well. He gave her all his money. "I don't want it, its yours," he would say but she used to save some of it and everytime they went to a town that had a bank she would put the money into an account in his name. But she never told him of what she was doing. They stayed with the Von Gattor circus for the next six years. Here Cilo learnt his trade.

Martin Galley one of the biggest circuses of that time then

asked Cilo to join them as the top name of the circus bill. But before Clio could make up his mind Von Gattor fell dead. Deep down he did not want to leave the circus he had grown up in, but now Von Gattor was dead he, Cara and Comeko joined Martin Galley's circus. It was another step up the ladder for young Cilo. He was now sixteen years old and he had started to do his own tricks with the help of Comeko. He asked if his two other friends, Miko and Diko the other clowns could join him and they did. Von Gattor's circus was no more since Von Gattor himself had died no one had wanted to take it over so it closed down.

Martin Galley's circus was not like Von Gattor's. It was almost twice the size with many animals and people working and acting in the show. Cilo could not get enough of the circus, he lived and breathed it and would have died for it. It was his life and as always by his side was Cara watching and loving him. If you upset Cilo you paid for it, Cara would be after you! Wherever he went Cara went, meetings, dinner dates, shows, holidays and just like at Von Gattor's circus crowds they all went mad over him. Girls almost threw themselves at him and he loved it.

It was not until he was twenty-one years old that by chance he found his gift that was to make him the greatest clown of all times. His gift was *tears* and in the papers he was known as the *Clown of Tears*.

Martin Galley was a very rich American who not only owned the circus but was a partner in a large shipping company and owned a great deal of land in Texas, property in Boston, New York and Washington. He watched Cilo's act many times and knew here was a money maker. A boy with a great talent who would go right to the top with a little help. Martin Galley was that help. Martin and Cilo became very close and great friends and through Martin all Cilo's dreams were to come true. Martin paid Cilo top money and helped him invest his money so that it would grow to secure his future.

With Cilo was his old friend Comeko, Brandy an American clown, and Peppi from Malta. They all worked hard on Cilo's act, but it came easy to Cilo – his timing was spot on, running, falling, laughing, crying were perfect. They all loved him and he in return loved them all. It was a great team for now there were six of them in the act. The new team had started at a friend's house when Lady Burmoth, who had just arrived from England, was giving a party and wanted some entertainment for her guests. Cilo's name was mentioned plus a country singer, guitarist and a piano player. It was the first very big party Cilo had ever gone to but he would not go unless his five friends and of course Mother Cara could go too. So everyone was invited to the party. Everyone wanted to meet Cilo before he left, as in a few weeks he was off to America to work and live.

After the country singer the clowns performed their act. Part of it was that Brandy was to tell Cilo his little dog had ran off and they could not find him. The dog's name was Cherry. Cilo was to look very sad so everyone would say, "Ahhh" then make out to cry. Cilo looked at all the guests with a very sad face, head down and started to cry. Built into his costume, behind his ears, were small tubes and by pressing buttons inside both pockets they would push water through the tubes, which would then run down his cheeks. But when Cilo pressed the buttons nothing happened. No water, no tears - a poor act. He tried again but nothing, no water. He felt sick inside as this was the first time this part of the act had gone wrong. He was on stage on his own and everyone was looking at him waiting to see what he was going to do next.

After the show he said, "I remember saying 'Mother in Heaven help me!'" Then it happened. He started to cry. Tears ran down his face, lots of tears. He just stood there and did not know what to do. The people watching went mad, shouting, laughing and calling out, "Cilo, Cilo, Cilo, Cilo!" The noise was deafening. Then Brandy came back with a little pink poodle, he gave it to Cilo and again they all went mad. Cilo hugged the little dog kissed it and waved to everyone and walked off, turning around waving he was gone. How many times he was called back he lost count. Martin just looked at him and shook his head, "How does he do it? I'm looking at a legend!" he told his wife.

Three weeks later Cilo was on a boat on its way to America. He had never been on a boat before nor had Cara and they both loved it. It was while on the boat that he met Gemma, who in less than a year was to become his wife of sixty-eight years. In that time they had eight children, four boys and four girls. Gemma was with her mother and a school friend going back home to America to a place called Lewistown in Montana. They had stayed at her mother's sister's home in Catania, Sicily for three months and had loved every minute of their holiday. Gemma was eighteen years old and was thinking of becoming a nurse when her holiday was over and she was back in America. That was until she met Cilo. She had gone to the circus and seen Cilo but meeting him on the boat without his make-up on she had no idea who he was. It was love at first sight for both of them.

They had been given the same table for the trip back to America but more than that, seats next to each other. Again luck was on Cilo's side for Gemma's mum also liked him and got on really great with Cara and they were to become close friends for the rest of their lives. Cilo had told Cara and his friends not to say a word to anyone as to whom he was, especially Gemma, but it did not take long before everyone knew that he was a passenger on board the *Princess Grace*. For the rest of the trip he was signing this bit of paper, this book cover, that scrap book, but he enjoyed every minute of it. When Gemma found out who Cilo was she said to her mother, "I knew there was something about him! Of all the people I fall in love with it had to be a clown."

"Well if nothing else he will always make you laugh!" And for the next sixty-eight years that's what he did. They had one of the longest marriages in show business and their love for each other got stronger as the years passed.

Whilst they were on the boat Cilo and his friends worked on their new act that was being planned across America. It was to start off in New York and be there for four weeks. If all went well they were to stay for another two weeks but they would have to wait and see. "We must have the best acts in our show, for our show must be number one in the world." So many great names were called and most of them jumped at being asked to join Cilo's circus. It took quiet a long time to put together the show but at last it was ready to go.

The New York tickets were all sold out in less than twenty-four hours. Cilo could not believe it for the next four weeks every ticket sold in less than twenty-four hours.

"This must be a record," Martin said. "I think you've made it Cilo!" And they all laughed. "It's going to be a lot of hard work, but knowing you, you will love every minute of it."

With that they all clapped hands and shouted, "Let the paint go on and wheels roll!"

"Drinks are on me!" Cilo said.

"What are we waiting for?" Martin shouted out. "Let's go before he changes his mind." So it was a good night out and it lasted well into the early hours of the morning.

The next day in his office Martin sat talking to Cilo and Cara, "Contracts are all ready to sign." So they signed, shook hands and paint and wheels were ready to roll.

Martin continued, "The ten shows across America are: one in New York, two in Pittsburgh Pennsylvania, three Ohio, four Indiana, five Illinois, six Missouri, seven Kentucky, eight West Virginia, nine Baltimore, and ten Philadelphia. The tour will take a year and if at the end all goes well, and, of course, after a rest,

I have been offered another ten states. But we will see. Also they want to film your show Clio. We open in New York on the 24th March. I want to have a word with you. The Capo six asked if they could go on in the second half of the show."

"I'll leave it to you Martin, I've got so much going on," Cilo said as he and Cara got up to leave.

This is how the acts of Cilo's circus show line up:

First there was *Ponti and his performing dogs.* You would not believe what his dogs could do, the children loved them. There were ten and some would not do as they were told. Some played football, others rode small ponies, others ran on top of large beach balls, some would skip. They did so many funny things and of course whatever the dogs did or did not do was part of the act. Ponti was simply the best. He came from Italy.

Then there was *The Great Maggon.* You could not believe what you saw or what he did with birds, rabbits, paper and many other things that he used in his act. The Great Maggon came from France.

And then, *Lady Cremma and her troopers.* Eight beautiful white horses, four small ponies and one goat. What a display of horsemanship, a breathtaking act. Lady Cremma came from Spain.

Next in the act came *Cilo and friends.* Without a doubt the greatest clowns in the world. Their timing, tricks, talking to the audience, fooling about and of course Cilo, were magic to watch. The audience just went mad over him so they came on twice, first half and then as last act of the show when he would cry. Cilo was from Sicily and his friends from varying places.

The fifth act was *Papa Caso and his flying six.* They were the greatest acrobatic family in the world and they could do things up there on the high wire that you would never believe. Cilo gave them what they wanted for he knew a happy team was a good team and his team was the best in the world and he wanted it to stay that way. Papa Caso and his flying six were from Poland.

Markoff Degillan'e was a knife thrower. Not just any knife thrower but a bowman, rifle man, whip lasher, axe thrower and anything else he could get his hands on to throw. His partner was Meeka Degillan'e, his tiny wife. When Markoff threw you could hear a pin drop in the audience. Everything he threw or fired was aimed at his tiny wife who stood at four feet ten tall. The speed and accuracy was mind blowing. Markoff and Meeka Degillan's came from Romania.

The list was went on, but every act was the best in its field, second to none. All together there were to be ten acts in his three hour show. Cilo was so happy that he rang Gemma and asked her to marry him and then announced, "My life is complete."

And of course Gemma had said "Yes."

The papers were full of Cilo and his circus. Day in and day out he was in the papers - you would think people would get sick of him but they could not get enough of him. He opened this and opened that, even opened his own clown school in New York and in less than a week there was a waiting list to join. It was crazy. And all the time Cara kept his feet on the ground, she was the boss and Cilo would have it no other way.

CILO THE CLOWN
He's small, he's not tall
He's tall to those who are small,
He dreams of lions, tigers and bears,
Of climbing up ladders and falling off chairs.
He wears long boots and a funny hat,
His coat is of red and pants of green.
He's the funniest clown you've ever seen.

He gets chased by a pig, gets chased by a donkey,
And tells the crowd her name is Honkey, Honkey the donkey,

He loves Mumma Cara and his babies of eight,
But the love of his life is his Gemma his soul mate.

They say up in Heaven the Lord God waits,
The circus is ready the lights are aglow,
And the angels are waiting for Cilo to show.
He's made many laugh over the years,
And he will always be known as the Clown of Tears.

This poem was written about Clio, but even today no one knows who wrote it. It just dropped in his letterbox after his death. Over his many years on this earth Cilo met many great and famous people. Presidents of the United States, the King of England, Duchesses, Barons, Earls, the King of Spain, many Kings and Queens, Dukes, Lords, Ladies and many, many film stars. Hunters, boxers, Lord Taxmore of Havant, the explorer Carl Morgan, the deep sea diver Penta, the famous guitarist Donamega and Carmanda the Spanish dancers, Johnny Weismuller (Tarzan) and even Hitler. Everyone who was famous wanted to say they knew him. Everyone wanted to know him rich or poor and he was mobbed everywhere he went. He toured the world many times and every time he loved doing it. As long as he was involved in the circus he was happy, very happy. Before nearly every show he would go out into the streets and give ten free tickets away to the poor who could not afford to go and see his show. His tour took him to all over the world to England, France, New Zealand, Turkey, Holland, Spain, Australia, Italy, Norway, Finland, Sweden, Denmark and of course Sicily his birth place.

He could make people laugh just by listening to him speak in his broken English for he would say, "I can not understand what I say myself sometimes!" and he would burst out laughing. In the 1914/1918 War he did his bit, entertaining troops and again in the Second World War he entertained many soldiers, sailors and airmen all over the world. And they loved him for it. He worked with Bing Crosby, Bob Hope, Glen Miller and many more singers, dancers and famous film stars.

He had a very full life, although tiring sometimes as as soon as he finished one tour he was off on another. He loved working with Al Jolson, Fred Astare and was a great friend of Big John, John Wayne.

It was now 1947 and Cilo was fifty-seven years old and still working non-stop. Cara was dying, she was eighty-seven years old, but when you first met her you could not guess her age. She would say, "I cannot go yet, some one has got to keep and eye on him, keep his feet on the ground. He's been my life, I love him so. He is my son, if I ever had a son it would have to be Cilo or none at all. God was good to me he gave me what man could not, my Cilo." And on the morning of July 8th 1947 Cara passed away in her sleep.

Cilo's world fell apart. She was his mother, friend, nurse, partner, advisor and she was the boss. He loved her so much his heart was broken. He cried and cried.

"How can I go on without her?" he said to Gemma.

"You must, as she wants you to. You know that I have a letter for you from Cara. She asked me to give it to you after she had died. She knew she did not have long to live but did not want to say anything of how ill she was. Even right up to her death she was thinking of you Cilo. Don't let her down in life. She never let you down, think well for you know I speak the truth." And Cilo knew all Gemma said was so very true. So he went out into his garden sat alone and read Cara's last letter to him. By just opening it the tears came, he could not stop them, did not want to stop them as they were tears of love, sadness, memories of all the years they had spent together, from boy to man, man to father, from little lost boy to famous clown. And it was all made possible by Mother Cara who fussed over him like an old mother hen, and deep down he loved every minute of it . He had loved it for almost all of his life. But now she was gone. It took a long time to get over Cara's death, some say he never did. In our story I've mentioned Cilo's sister called Caddeka. She had been killed falling off a horse three weeks before her thirteenth birthday although Cilo did not know of his sister's death for almost a year. So by the time he was almost twelve himself he had lost a mother, father and sister. Was it God's was of sending Cara to love and look after him through his life? I think so. His old world was gone when Cara came his new world was just starting. And what a new world! Cara was to make sure of that and she was right. Up to the day of her own life coming to an end.

The letter to Cilo read:

July 1947

To my son,

In our life together there has been many things I've done of which you were not too happy about, starting when you were a boy at Von Gattor's circus, when you let the monkeys out of their cage because Von Gattor would not let you go and help feed the tiger. I told you off when you punched Capo for laughing at you when you fell off Timo's horse and made him cry. I stopped you from helping clean the horses out and made you do your homework. I know how you felt, it hurt me to do these things but you had to learn if you were to grow up a good, honest man. You have to give and take in this life. There were many times I told you off for this or that but if you look back then look at yourself this day, it is good I did these things.

Then there was the contract with George Grapps. I would not sign for he was not a good man you would have lost much money, but you got upset. Again I had to do this. Many times over the years I've said no but only for your good. George Grapps is now spending many years in jail for his twisting people out of their money. That's what mothers and fathers do while their children are growing up and one day you will do the same for your children, if not you then Gemma.

Thank you Cilo for so many wonderful years spent together, you gave

137

me so much happiness and love I thank God for giving me you in my life, you gave me reason to live. So now I give you a reason to live on, even though my life is now over. Yours has a long way to go. Only one thing I ask of you, don't forget me. I'll always be there for you even though I'm in the next world, our two worlds are very close. Everyday of my life on this earth I used to say a prayer to God, I would say to him thank you for my Cilo. But now I'm with my Lord God I will say thank you Lord for both of us for every second of happiness he gave us. Cilo be a good boy, live a good honest life like I bought you up to do. Cilo if you ever have a problem tell me of it as I will listen son. I love you very much. May God always walk with you. Don't forget your prayers and don't throw your dirty clothes on the bathroom floor like you usually do! I'll be watching you.

Loving you always Mother.

Cilo read and read Cara's letter many times and many years on he would read it many times more. It was the first time Cara had left the word Cara out when she sent him a letter or note it ended with loving you always Mother Cara. But not her last letter. Cilo just cried and cried as he missed her so badly and loved her so much. He sat in the garden for a long, long time. Gemma left him on his own as he needed time and space to himself. She would now and then look out to make sure that he was okay. During their long marriage they had eight children four of each. After their last child was born he said, "To have four children of each God is good to us it is time we stopped having babies!" These are the names of his eight children girls first - Shaneto, Berika, Coran, baby Bella, Niko, Keba, Casame, Bernado. Cilo noticed that there was not date on the letter just he month and year. He knew that she had known she was dying but did not know how long she had and she never said a word to him. Slowly Cilo got back to his love, being a clown and over the next twenty-five years travelled all over the world. But time was catching up with him, he could not run into the ring, climb ladders and do many of his old tricks. But just to be there in the circus was enough for the crowds as long as they could see and hear him talk to them they went home happy, very happy. Here are some of the things he did in his act:

First the ringmaster would come into the ring, there would be a box on one side of the ring that two men carried in as the ring master walked round the ring shaking hands with the crowd the box would start to follow him. All you could see were two bright green small legs. When the ringmaster looked round the box would stand still, in the end the ringmaster chased the box and the crowd knew it. He'd run in the ring doing cartwheels, ride on his donkey (Honkey) slide down a rope into the ring, you never knew what he would do next or where he would appear from. You would be watching the show and next thing he would be sitting next to you, pull you out into the ring and play about then as you left the ring he'd give you two free tickets for the show and for that they went wild with delight. At the end of the show they would call his name out many times and many times he would come back out. His record was fifteen call outs and he loved everyone.

In 1972 that he was invited back to Sicily and made a Lord by his President, over his long years as a clown he had been given many honours, but this was the icing on the cake for Cilo and Gemma, it was in every newspaper round the world. Cilo was now eighty-two years old, he was semi-retired but still very much involved in the circus. He had seen many of his friend pass-on. There were so many laws can't do this, can't do that, have to have permits for the animals, that the circus that Cilo loved and knew was changing fast. In 1974 through back problems Cilo decided to call it a day and take a back seat. His children had grown up and were doing their own things, some married, Shanto married with two girls and living in France, his family had split up but kept in touch. They rang Cilo and Gemma every week and had lots of get together's during the year. Cilo and Gemma were grandparents nineteen times over. Only one child was not married and that was their last born, Bella. She was a doctor in England and did not want to get married for another two years her boyfriend was also a doctor. Cilo now spent most of his time visiting hospitals, old peoples homes, schools and doing social work. He and Gemma loved it and slowly the last few years slipped away. He sold all his rights to the circus in 1977. In 1978 they made a film about his life, many books were written about him. By the end of 1979 Cilo was not a well man, he could not walk, had trouble breathing but could still make you laugh. Many of his friends used to say, "Just listening to him talk in that funny accent made you laugh!" He could never master the English language and when he got upset he would revert back to Sicilian. They used to have a saying in Cilo's circus just before opening the show they would say, "Put the paint on and let the wheels roll." It meant everything was ready. It was also the name of the book about his life. Cilo said, "I was born in Sicily in 1890 and I would love to go home and die in Sicily." So in 1980 Cilo flew back home it was April 21st. He was now very ill, Gemma was now a very frail old lady, their children were all in Sicily as they knew their father was dying and time was running short. Two weeks after returning home Cilo Cakari died in his sleep on May 6th 1980, he was ninety years old in all his life after being made a Lord he never used Lord on his letters he just signed them Cilo Cakari. And sad to say on the 20th May 1980 Gemma also died in her sleep. They say she died because she loved Cilo so much that she gave up the will to live. So somewhere high in the heavens, Cilo, Cara and Gemma are getting ready for the greatest show on Earth to begin but this time the Lord God and the Angels will be watching.

Someone shouted, "Put the paint on and let the wheels roll."

Cilo put in his will, "I just want you to inscribe on my stone – Cilo Cakari Clown of Tears."

It was told that when Cilo died Gemma said, "Look my Cilo he has come back to say 'Good bye'" For Cilo was crying tears.

He truly was the Clown of Tears.

She Wolf

At the edge of the forest was a field and a path ran between the forest and the field, for this story is about She Wolf.

Walking along this pass was an old man dressed all in black. He had long grey hair, a long grey beard and he was wearing a large bed cap, hat or beret or something similar, but the back came down to his shoulders with markings on the front of it. He was walking slowly as if he was listening to the sounds around him. He stopped and turned round as if someone had called him. He lifted his hands up in front of him. His hands and fingers were long and thin and almost white. On his right hand second finger he wore a very large crystal ring. He pointed his ring at a large tree some twenty yards away, for behind the tree hiding was a man. Suddenly from the ring came energies of coloured rays – blue, silver, white. They came from the ring so fast and so many, so bright that you had to shield your eyes. Then the energy from the ring stopped. The man behind the tree could not move for the rays made him unable to.

Merlin came to the man and said, "Why do you follow me, as I know you wish me no harm? What is your name and tell me of your time and why do you hide from me?"

"I am Tom Cartwell a farmhand from Anton Hill Village. My wife is with child but cannot move and I am afraid she may die. I was told of you, that you can help us!"

"Yes, I can, but you must do what I say. If you do not, your wife with child may die."

"I will do whatever you say Merlin."

"Do you have others in your family?"

"Yes I have another child who is deaf, cannot speak or walk."

Merlin said, "Pick laeen berry, only the green one, elm leaves, toadstool, some river plant miras and get some goats milk and then boil in a large pot. Let it boil for five hours, strain the juice and give it to your wife morning, noon and night for three days and once more she will move and her child will move within her for she will soon give birth."

"But how do you know?"

At that Merlin walked away.

When Merlin was gone Tom found he could move again. He ran home and did everything that Merlin had told him and in three days his wife was well and could move about.

Soon Mavis gave birth to a little boy and they called him Tom.

Tom and Mavis had another child, a seven year old girl called Kathana. She could not talk, was deaf and a cripple. All she did was to sit by the door and cuddle a rag doll. It never left her and whatever she did she would not let her rag doll out of her arms. She really loved it. She was born with these ills and it was so sad for Mavis and Tom to see her this way, for the rest of her life there was nothing they could do for her.

About a week after little Tom's birth, Kathana had a dream. In her dream she saw Merlin calling her, telling her to go to Wolf Hill and he would be waiting for her. A Grafam Horse would take her to Wolf Hill. She had the same dream for seven nights.

On the eighth day her father signed to her that he and Mavis would be away for a few hours and off they went.

At Wolf Hill she felt as though someone was lifting her off the Grafam and putting her down on the grass. She did not know if she was dreaming or if it was real. But whatever it was, she was at Wolf Hill. Suddenly a wolf came walking towards her it sat down and just looked at her. Then came another wolf, and another, until there were about twenty all round her, just looking at her. She was not afraid of the wolves and she felt that she knew of Merlin even though she had never seen or heard of him.

Then a voice said, "Hello Kathana."

She looked around and there standing in front of her was an old man dressed in black, with a long grey beard and long grey hair. "I am known by the name of Merlin of Camarourn–Toggouras–De Ni."

Kathana noticed that the first wolf was not there. Merlin spoke to her again. She could hear every word he said to her! It was strange, for it was the first time she had heard anything in her world.

"Kathana you must stay here with the wolves, they will not harm you. When the wolves cry to the moon you will cry with them and when the wolves run you will run with them, for you will be of them. You will eat, sleep and play with them. Zaco is the pack leader and soon you will know the ways of the wolves as you are of them and they are of you for all time." Merlin looked at Kathana. "Do you hear what I say?"

"Yes Merlin."

"From this day on you will be known as Ramolin, the She Wolf of For-Linka Caryan Bue. For when the winds blow you will hear my voice and my command."

Merlin turned to the wolves and said, "Go my friends," and the wolves left. When she looked back at Merlin he was gone, but the first wolf was back and sat looking at her. Then the wolf got up looked to the forest then back at Kathana, as if to say follow me. She did but she was no longer a girl but a wolf.

Kathana was never seen again only at night. You could hear her cry to the moon for Merlin had said, "It is better to be as free as the wolves than to be chained as a human. So I gave her freedom."

KATHANA

She could not walk she could not talk,
Her life was hell her pain was many,
To run like the wolf to cry to the moon,
Was the wish of Merlin of Camaourn –
Toggouras – Di Ni Noon
So on that day on that hour she Kathana
Became a wolf instead of a dying flower.

MERLIN

Merlin did not live Merlin did not die
He did not laugh and he did not cry
He was not old nor was he young
He was of wolf he was of deer
He was of the forest stream that ran slow and clear
He was of the forest he was of the sky
He was the owl that could fly
He was the crow he was the rat
He was at times a wild cat
He was of no man or of time and place
He was a spirit from outer space!

The Case Of The Richmond Five

This is a funny little story of five old people who lived in an old people's home in the West Country just after 1939 – 1945 Second World War. Our story starts on the 8th September 1960. You may not think it funny after you have read the story.

Today old people's homes are called rest homes. Anyway, in this rest home there were fourteen elderly persons, but we are only interested in five of them. The five were Mrs Hanna Ball, Mr Li Cho, Mr Ackamo, Mr Boris Egor Hickerman and Miss Eria Ana Evoken (Ball England, Li Cho China, Keyo Acamo Japan, Hickerman Germany and Evoken Russia). They all had nick names for each other. Ball was Jumble, Ackamo was Sue'e, Li Cho was Tiddly, Hickerman was JB and Evoken was Vok.

I'm going to start our story, as I said, on the 8th September 1960. The weather was warm for that time of year. It was still very hot and every day the five would have breakfast in the garden, plus dinner, tea and sometimes supper. They always sat together. No one else was allowed to sit on their table or join the group. They did everything together and spent most of the days together. Their ages started at seventy and went up to eighty-two, and, for their ages, they were all very fit and well and happy old people. Behind their backs at the Home they were called by the nurses 'The Secret Five', for if you got too near them they would stop talking but as soon as you moved away they would start up again.

In their own funny way they were famous in the home as everyone outside and inside the home knew of the Secret Five. The nurses would just look at them huddled up and laugh and carry on with what they were doing. One morning Mrs Appleby, the Rest Home manager, was very upset and angry as someone had broken into her office and stolen files from her cabinet. Five altogether and the five files were those of the Secret Five. No one had seen or heard anything during the night and it was all very strange. Who would want to steal five old people's files? It did not make sense but they were gone from the cabinet. These files were marked 'private and confidential' and had things about the Secret Five that only the home knew about.

Mrs Appleby said to the Matron, "How did they get into my office? Only you and I have the keys. Why just take five why not take the whole lot? And another thing, there was a lot of money in my drawer and its still there, every penny! How did they get into my cabinet? Again only you and I have the keys and we carry them on us all the time. It's very strange and disturbing to think that someone can break into my office whenever they want and take what they want. I'll have the locks changed as soon as possible. It's not good what's happened for it could be anyone working here. I don't know whether to call the police or not.

"I think the best thing to do at the moment is to see if we can find the files first. Don't say a word about them to anyone yet."

"Matron, I'll leave it up to you to tell the nurses to check every room. Say we are looking for stolen money taken from the office while the door was open at breakfast this morning. And in the meantime we will just listen, watch and wait to see if the files do turn up!"

So it was agreed. The Matron said she would start the search right away. Mrs Appleby returned to her office and got on the phone to the locksmiths. The Matron went to each nurse and told them of the missing money. "Don't say a word to any of the residents. Be very careful as I don't want anyone to know that their room has been searched."

But after every room was searched nothing was found. The nurses looked every place you couldpossibly hide something.

"I'll give it until the end of the week and if nothing turns up I think I will call the police. Well at least I've got all new locks put on, in fact I've had two put on my office door," announced Mrs Appleby.

But at the end of the week the files were still missing and Mrs Appleby was still no nearer to finding them than when she first knew that they were stolen. "I'll call the police in on Monday morning as we are at the weekend. You never know they might turn up by then." But they never did.

On Monday morning Mrs Appleby called the police. She got a call back saying that Detective Inspector Tom Price would call in first thing on Tuesday morning. At 9'o clock sharp the police arrived.

"Sorry about yesterday, I was in court all day. This is Sergeant George Burns my partner. Do you want to start from the beginning? George will take notes."

So Mrs Appleby told the Inspector everything.

"Where are the five whose files are missing?" the Inspector asked after Mrs Appleby had finished.

"In the garden. You can see them from my window"

"Ah yes I see them."

Mrs Appleby said, "I do have another set of files on people who used to live here during the war, it was Government regulation to keep them. And I have duplicate files on every one living here now."

"Great, can you get them please and let's see if we can sort this out. Only five files taken?"

"Yes."

"Everything else still there?"

"Yes."

"Money?"

"Yes."

"The nine other residents files still there?"

"Yes."

"Are you sure nothing else was taken?"

"Yes."

"Good. Now let's move on to stage two. The duplicate files of the five missing files. Who's first? No, let's start with the first person out of the five to move in.

"Mrs Hanna Ball, born on February the 19th 1890 in England, so now aged seventy years old. Place of birth Brighton, Sussex. Married Richard Ball on October 3rd 1937 in Liverpool, husband RAF pilot killed – shot down over Germany flying a Wellington bomber on January 11th 1943. Richard Ball was stationed at Scammon Air base, Liverpool. He also lived in Brighton, Sussex. Hanna Ball, maiden name was Grey, not long married..." Mrs Appleby read.

"So sad the war took many young lives!" the Inspector said. "Anything else?"

"No, only she came here on June 30th 1950. Sshe went and stayed with her sister after her husband was killed. Her sister's husband knew Mr Alan Richmond, the owner of the Home so that is how she came to live here"

"What kind of person is Mrs Ball?"

"Very deep, but friendly. She likes walking and likes people around her."

"Any children?"

"No."

"Is that it?"

"I think so."

"Good. Who's next?"

"Miss Eria Evoken, born in Russia in 8th February 1891 in

Novor just outside Novorossiysk, a small Russian port in the Black sea. Aged sixty-nine years old, never married, came to England via Spain in 1934, lived in Birkenhead, Lancashire and worked for a local paper. Very good English, she worked as a typist and part time reporter, also very good with figures. Oh, I've just remembered... they all, I mean the five, have nicknames. Mrs Ball is Jumble and Miss Evoken is Vok."

"Thank you."

"Miss Evoken came to the home on July 30th 1950... said she was told by a friend who read about us in the paper War Cry and it is true we did advertise in that paper at that time"

"Any children?"

"Not as I know."

"Thank you. What kind of person is she?"

"If she gets upset she will shout a lot in Russian. She does not like the cold and she can out-eat every person in the home! Gets on well with the staff and the rest of the residents."

"That's all?"

"Yes, I think so."

"Good."

"Number three is Mr Keyo Ackamo from Japan, born Kobe 1890 as far as we know on June 7th. We only know what he tells us. He came to England 1940, exact date not known, lived in Bootle worked in an arms factory all through the war. Very good English, came to England via Germany and France - he said the Germans were rounding up all foreigners and his name was on their list. He came over on a small cargo boat, was investigated and found clean. Came to the Home August 28th 1950. He said he decided to move down to the West Country for his health and got to hear about us. Plays chess and is very good. No one has ever beaten him yet! Reads a lot and likes short walks. Never stays up late always in bed by 10'o clock seven days a week. No trouble, very polite..."

"Any more?"

"No that's it."

"Good. And his nickname, I take it he's got one?"

"Yes its Toe."

"Toe?"

"Don't ask me why, I haven't got a clue. The only people who know are the other four of the five."

"Okay thanks."

"Next."

"Mr Li Cho."

"Chinaman?"

"Yes."

"Carry on."

"Mr Cho is the youngest of the five. He was born in Peking China in 1895 on the 10th May then came to England with his parents in1910. Lived in Wellesley. Surprise! He trained at Liverpool College to become a schoolteacher, very good English. He also speaks German, Chinese, French and teaches German and French. He married a Chinese girl who also lived in Wellesley called May Loo in 1921 at Liverpool Registry office. Two children, both dead – one killed when the house was hit, the other knocked down by an army lorry. Wife also killed in an air raid. A very nervous man keeps looking around all the time. He doesn't say much and doesn't seem to fit in with the other four. Wears small glasses – his eyesight is bad. Came to the Home in December 1950, the17[th]. Moved to the West Country to take up a part time teachers' training course, heard about us and moved in as I said December 17th. He likes gardening, walks and a game of chess. His nickname is Tiddly."

"Tiddly? They get worse!"

"And the last one is Mr Boris Egor Hickerman. Born in Berlin 2nd March 1889. Father a doctor who left Germany with his family 1913 went to Holland to work and live. Mother died 1915 – blood clot to the brain. Family moved from Holland to England in 1921 to Woolton, where father worked at Liverpool General Hospital until he died of a heart attack in 1930. Boris Egor Hickerman the son trained to be a nurse at Liverpool General. Never married, no one knew if he was or wasn't. Moved to the home 19th December 1950. Bad-tempered man likes to bully and wants his own way - he has been warned behave or he will be asked to leave. Likes chess, playing cards and history on Germany. Nick name Herr Hit!"

"Is that is?"

"Yes."

"Good got it all down, George?"

"Yes sir!"

"Good. Now, can we have a look at your office. The door was not forced?"

"No."

"The window was not forced?"

"No."

"So whoever stole the five files used a key to get into your office and it was not your key or the key of Matron, is that right?"

"Yes."

"Good."

After looking around the office the Inspector said, "Thank you for your help. May I take the files with me?"

"Yes."

"Thank you. I will be in touch Mrs Appleby. Oh one thing, where was Matron on the night the files were stolen?"

"She and her husband were at my house for dinner and they stayed the night. I ran her home the next morning at 7'o clock."

"Thank you, that clears that up." And with that they left.

On the way back to the station the Inspector said to George, "Well George now stage three. What do you think?"

"Could be an inside job and the motive money."

"Could be blackmail, the five could have something to hide and our thief found out, for all five lived and worked around Liverpool at the same time. All five moved into the home in 1950. All five came from different countries and they stay together. I think this one George will need a lot of digging!"

"Yes sir."

It was court in the afternoon, the end of their last case. "Get this out the way and tomorrow we will look closer at our five friends. We could call this case 'The Secret Five', but it sounds like a child's book. What's the name of the Home George?"

"Richmond Care Home."

"Good. I think we will call this case the Richmond Five, what do you think?"

"Sounds okay to me."

"Good, then it's the case of the Richmond Five!"

The next morning sharp at 9'o clock the Inspector was in his office. George was waiting with toast and tea.

"Ahh good man. Morning!"

"Morning sir. I've got it all written up on the blackboard."

"Right now let's go over it all again. Five people – two women and three men. One English woman, one Russian, one Japanese man, one Chinese man and one German, yes?"

"Yes."

"Right all lived and worked in and around Liverpool, yes?"

"Yes."

"Good. And all at the same time?"

"Yes."

"Right and all five moved into Richmond Care Home between June and December 1950?"

"Yes."

"Right all born in 1890s?"

"Yes."

Female	Ball	born 1890	19th Feb	Hanna	England
Female	Evoken	born 1891	8th Feb	Eria Ana	Russia
Male	Ackamo	born 1890	7th June	Keyo	Japan
Male	Cho	born 1895	8th May	Li	China
Male	Hickerman	born 1893	2nd March	Boris Egor	Germany

"Hanna Ball... married?"

"Yes."

"Husband killed?"

"Yes."

"Eria Evoken... single?"

"Yes... well never married not as far as we know sir."

"Keyo Ackamo... single?"

"Yes. Never married not as far as we know sir"

"Li Cho... married?"

"Yes. Wife killed and two children both dead sir."

"Boris Hickerman single?"

"Yes, never marriedas far as we know sir"

"Now. Why would five people, all living and working around Liverpool at the same time, all living in the Care Home at the same time, moving in within six months of each other, all became very close to one another and want to keep themselves to themselves?"

"For coincidence sir?" They both laughed.

"Go make a pot of tea George. Why oh why and why only their five files missing? Why? What do we know about Liverpool? One – it's where a lot of troops were shipped out from during the war. Two – it has a very large shipping port. Three – it had a lot of factories making guns, ammunition, spitfires, tanks and bombers. Four – thousands of people worked in factories day and night. Five – it was bombed many times."

"Too many if you ask me sir."

"Yes, but so was Coventry, Birmingham and London. But let's get back to Liverpool. It holds the key to the case."

"Last night," George said, "I had a word with my dad. He said a lot of merchant ships loaded up with food, supplies for the Middle East, North Africa and a lot of other places. There were always ships in and out doing escort duty."

"No, that's not it. I think they could be spies!"

"Spies? Why do you say that?"

"I don't know. I've got a strange feeling about this one. Four out of the five countries were at war with England. Why Liverpool? Dig deeper, George. Was there something they were after in Liverpool or being made there?"

"Wait a minute sir. The Royal Navy were doing trials on a new submarine, it was being built in Liverpool. It was supposed to be hush-hush. This new sub was called XB(1), it could dive deeper, do more knots, was bigger, hold more tubes and had more crew, was harder to detect and could stay down for twice as long as any other sub."

"Who told you this?"

"Old Tom Carter. He was a Navy man on the subs and was stationed at Ferry Point Dock Yard – home of the subs!"

"Well, now we know why it was always being bombed. Well done George!"

"Thank you sir."

"Now we've got to find out if the five have anything to do with the subs and Liverpool and we must find the person who stole the files. We've got to find this person or persons for they hold the key. Were the five spies sending messages to Germany by code? We know each one was good at something, Hanna Ball knew all about the RAF movements, when bombings were to be, where they were going, how many bombers, time they took off and time they would get back and how many never came back."

"But she lost her husband on a bombing raid sir."

"Yes, I know. But was she blackmailed to work for Germany? After her husband was killed fall in love with one of the three men and spy for him to keep him? Did he use her?

"Erica Evoken was very good with figures and could speak English, German and French. Worked for a local paper. Single, she could spend her nights round the clubs and bars chatting up the sailors, airmen and soldiers for information. By her photo she was a good looking woman.

"Keyo Ackamo worked in an arms factory all through the war, speaks very good English. He could pick up lots of things in the factory that were going on. His files say that he used to mess about with wirelesses, repairing them and so could he have been the radio operator sending messages to Germany or some other place?

"Li Cho a school teacher..."

"Do you notice sir that they all speak German?"

"Yes I had noticed. Cho had use of the school phone. They say if you want to know something, ask a child. His files say that he was very good with children. Questions he could ask his class; 'what does your father do for a living?', get the child to open up, 'what does your mother, brother, sisters, uncles, aunts do?' It would give him a good picture and if one of the children's fathers or mothers were doing anything special he would get to know it by the child."

"Clever."

"If we are right, too clever. And the last one, our friend Boris Egor Hickerman, male nurse. Wounded men in his hospital, he could ask how they got wounded, get friendly with the injured and they would tell him what he wanted to know just by asking or offering to do things for them - post a letter, make a phone call, get cigarettes for them - just by doing favours for them.

"Put all their information together and bang you've got enough to code back to Germany!"

"Sounds good sir, all we've got to do is prove it."

"Easier said than done George. But its early days. I think I will go back to the Rest Home tomorrow and have a look at our five friends."

"Good idea sir."

"I want you to find out as much as you can about this sub."

"Yes sir."

"Good off you go."

By 2'o clock George was back in the office.

"Any luck George?"

"Think so sir. I looked up the records and I rang Captain Marshal. He helped me get through the red tape."

"Good. Right, what have you got?"

"Well sir in 1939 the Navy started work on a new sub and it was called J129, but later changed to the XB(1). This sub was all I said it was ... a very powerful weapon against the enemy. The German U boats would be no match for the XB(1). By April 1942 most of the trials were finished and they had it down for service in June 1942. She would slip away late at night to do trials then slip back into port again late the next night. Everything was going to plan."

"What date in June?"

"Well sir, the date was the 12th June but Churchill put a hold on it."

"Why?"

"Don't know, sir."

"Strange, but then Churchill was strange, but a very good war man."

"Getting back to the Germans, we knew that that they knew about the subs because they caught a German spy who had paper work on him about the sub."

"What did it have on it?"

"Not much just: 'He can run fast, dive deep stop don't sleep stop... code sort of sir, but enough to let the Navy know the Germans were on to them."

"Carry on."

"Well sir this is the part that you won't believe! Apparently, there never was a sub called XB(1) it was all a hoax. It was a ploy to get the Germans to put their top men into Liverpool. They knew most of the spy rings and knew every movement they made, they knew all their codes. But there was one man they wanted badly, he was in London somewhere and they wanted to get him to Liverpool so they could kill him. Knowing he would contact one of the four known spy rings in Liverpool, they would know just as soon as he made contact and go for him."

"But the sub? It went back to 1939?"

"Yes sir."

"But I don't understand, 1939 to be used to catch German spies in 1942. It doesn't make sense!"

"No sir."

"What else?"

"That's it."

"But there must be more."

"Sorry sir, the file is closed. Why they put it out in 1939 about a new sub and then used it in 1942 only the government know! But I was told whatever they had in mind it worked."

"Good, you've done well George. You'll make a policeman one day!" They both laughed. "Come I'll buy you dinner."

Then the phone rang and George answered it.

"Thanks that's great. . . thanks, I owe you one."

"Who was that?"

"The answer to our XB(1) mystery! Well sir in 1939 it seems they did start work on a new sub calling it J129, then the XB(1). But in 1940 they stopped work on it. And it was Churchill's idea to' 'bring it back to life' in Liverpool hoping to get the Germans to go looking for it. It would hurry them, and it worked. That's why he called it off, because there was really no sub. But then, as I said, they knew all the spy rings, so if they sent a message saying Merchant ships, say twenty, sailing on the 5th they would hold them back. Also the Germans would send as many agents as they could to find this so called super-sub."

"Clever, very clever. For that I'll buy you two teas." And the Inspector kept his word.

The next day they went back to the Home. "I think I would like a word with your staff Mrs Appleby, one at a time. Let's start in the kitchen with the cook," demanded the Inspector.

"That's Mrs Bowley, she's been with us from day one."

"Thank you, Mrs Appleby we will call you when we need you." The manager went back to her office.

"Ah, Mrs Bowley?" asked the Inspector

"Yes."

"I am Inspector Price and this is Sergeant Burns. Can we ask you a few questions?"

"What about?"

"About the Home and the people that live here."

"What do you want to know?"

"Is there anyone here that you don't particularly like?"

"Yes. The German, Mr Hickerman."

"Why?"

"He's a very rude man."

"Anyone else?"

"No just him."

"Do you see much of Mr Richmond, the owner of the home?"

"He pops in every now and then, you never know with him when he will come."

"What does he do?"

"When he's here? He talks a lot to the German."

"Does he speak German?"

"Yes, very well. If you listen to him you'd think he was a German!"

"What about the German's four other friends?"

"No. He just says 'hello' to Mrs Ball."

"Is that it?"

"Yes."

"How long does he stay?"

"Two days at the most."

"When was the last time you saw him?"

"About a month ago, saying that Molly…"

"Who's Molly?"

"She's the part time nurse. She does two night a week. She said she saw his car at the back of the Black Bull."

"Black Bull?"

"It's a pub about half a mile from here."

"When did she see his car?"

"About eight to ten days ago."

"Where is Molly now?"

"She'll be in bed - she was on nights last night."

"Have you any children Mrs Bowley?"

"Yes, two boys."

"What does your husband do?"

"He works on the docks."

"It's been nice talking to you. Goodbye."

And they left the kitchen.

"I think we will have a chat with Molly and find out more about our Mr Richmond."

They went back to Mrs Appleby's office. "I need to talk to Molly. Is it possible? I know she was on nights last night."

"Yes, you're in luck. She will be in today in about an hour's time to pick up her wages."

"Good. Meanwhile, we will have a look around if that's alright?"

"Yes."

"Good." And the policemen went on a tour of the Rest Home until they got word that Molly was in.

Molly was about sixty years old, small and thin. A good looking woman for her age.

"We would like to ask a few questions. Do you mind?"

"No."

"Good. How long have you worked here?"

"Five years."

"Like it?"

"Yes."

"Are you married?"

"Yes."

"Any children?"

"Yes, three girls."

"What does your husband do?"

"He's a foreman at Cox's Builders Merchants."

"Do you know, or see, Mr Richmond much?"

"I know him, but only as a boss."

"Don't you talk to him?"

"No, only to say 'hello'."

"Does he come in here a lot?"

"About every two months or so he just turns up."

"When was the last time you saw him?"

"About two weeks ago. Well, I didnt see him, I saw his car behind the Black Bull pub. He was probably in the pub."

"How did you know it was his car?"

"He has a Rialy, black in colour and there's a bumper missing off his front bumper, if you know what I mean."

"What side?"

"Driver's side."

"Are you sure?"

"Yes, I've seen his car many times over the years I've worked here."

"Now when did you see his car?"

"Let's see. It was the night old Billy Contan died, and that was ten days ago. I was on my way home from his house . . . yes, it was Monday night the 30th August."

"What time?"

161

"About half past nine. The car was gone when I passed the pub Tuesday morning."

"What time?"

"About 10'o clock. Why are you asking all these questions?"

"Some money was stolen from Mrs Appleby's office while everyone was at breakfast."

"Oh yes, I heard about that. Terrible, can't trust anyone these days."

"Thanks for your help."

"Now what?" George asked when Molly had gone.

"I think I know our thief. But if it was him, then why?"

Luck was on their side again for Mrs Appleby informed them that Mr Richmond had rung to say he would be at the Home at around 4'o clock.

"Let's go get something to eat and wait for Mr Richmond!" He arrived just after 4'o clock.

"Mr Richmond, the police would like to have a word with you," Mrs Appleby told him.

"What for?"

"I don't know sir."

"Thank you." Then he saw the Inspector walking toward him, "How can I help you?"

"Just making a few inquiries sir."

"About what?"

"The break in, in Mrs Appleby's office."

"It's nothing, its not important. I'll sort it out internally anyway. I'll be here for a few days. Thank you for calling."

"Before we go I want to ask you some questions. You don't live at the Home I understand?"

"No."

"But you have your own room here?"

"Yes"

"You live in Liverpool?"

"Yes."

"Can we have the address?"

"Why?"

"In case we want to talk to you."

"Ohh."

"Do you mind?"

"No."

"Thank you. Do you speak German?"

"Yes."

"French?"

"Yes."

"Dutch?"

"No."

"What kind of work are you in?"

"I've retired."

"How old are you sir?"

"I was born in 1900, that makes me sixty"

"You look very fit for a sixty year old."

"Thank you."

"Do you still drive?"

"Yes."

"What car do you drive?"

"A Rialy."

"Nice car!"

"I think so. Anything else Inspector?"

"No."

"Then may I leave as I have got a lot of things to do before I go back to Liverpool?"

"Thank you for your help sir."

"Horrible piece of work, if you don't mind me saying so," George said once they were out side. "He never told you what he used to work at."

"I know, but I already know!"

"You do?"

"Yes."

"What?"

"He owned a shop. Guess what kind of shop?"

"Wireless shop?"

"Yes ... and what else?"

"Give up sir!"

"Cameras!"

"I should have guessed!"

"You should have. It's all falling into place now. Let's get back to the office, I've got some more to put on our blackboard."

"Right. Alan Richmond age sixty years old being born on the 29th January 1900, in Liverpool General Hospital. Found unfit for services in the armed forces. Not much known about him until he was asked to be a part-time policeman. Part of his duties was to escort ... wait for it ... spies that were caught! And at the beginning quite a few were caught. He opened a shop in Leyton Road, Liverpool in 1940 and closed down in 1944. He opened the Rest Home in 1949 with Mrs Appleby and a Dr Ben Zigaman. Dr Zigaman died after falling under a car in 1950 or rather was hit by a car for the car did not stop!"

"Right. I want you to dig deep into the accident, find out all you can."

"Where was the accident?"

"Tavistock."

"Tavistock?"

"Yes."

"Date of the accident?"

"November 30th 1950."

"I'll get on to it right away sir!"

"Good this case is getting deeper as the days go by. We could have here murder, spies, break-in, five people keeping together. What else will come up? Fake sub?" All this went through the Inspector's mind as there was a knock at the door. It was his boss.

"How's things going Tom?"

"So so. Getting there."

"Good. I want you to take over the Goodman murder. Jack is in hospital could be there some time."

"Hope to wrap this one up in a few days."

"Right. Take over Jack's case on Monday. That gives you four days. Regards to Betty!" And he was gone.

It was time to go home. As the Inspector was putting his topcoat on George walked into the office. "Ahh you're back, got much?"

"No sir. No witnesses, body was found by a local bobby, Pc Matfield John at 11.20pm on the corner of Oak Tree Lane and Farway Road. The doctor was dead, looked like a hit and run. If it was a lorry, the lorry driver might not have known he had hit someone."

"Possibly," the Inspector said. "Go on."

"That's about it. Oh, one other thing. A young lad tried to sell car parts about a month later to a junk scrapyard for eight bob, one of the parts was off a Rialy car – a bumper, but it was in a mess, it looked as though a lorry had ran over it plus the rust had got at it."

"Pity. How do you know this?"

"The scrapyard was raided by the police. They had had a tip off that they were selling stockings and booze under the counter, found a sack with car parts still in it. Peter Mando said he had parts stolen off his motor bike and was asked to go down the station to see if any of his bike gear was in the sack. He found his mirror and noticed the bumper. The police asked what car the bumper could have come off and he told them a Raily."

"End of story, George?"

"End of story sir, what now?"

"Home. Goodnight George."

"Goodnight sir."

It was Thursday morning at the station.

"Are you going to talk to the five at the Home sir?" George asked.

"No. I was, but I'm not going to for the moment."

"Any reason?"

"Yes. Leave them to stew! They know we've been at the Home, talked to Mrs Appleby, the cook, night nurse and Mr Richmond would have told them if he was the thief and the five were spies. He would know he was their boss!"

"Did he want to keep them all together so he knew where they were? Was he their boss but they did not know and somehow worked it so they all ended up at the Rest Home, all within six months of each other?"

"I'll take the first one, he was their boss and they knew it, did all their coded messages from his shop, probably had a basement."

"But why steal all their files knowing there are duplicates, it doesn't make sense?"

"No, I must admit I can't work that one out, but being his Home made it a lot easier for him. Plus I bet he had his Rest Home put in the Liverpool paper the War Cry, the rest was up to the five to make up a story to get into the Home. He being the owner would interview them."

"Did they ever catch the Master spy they were after sir?"

"No, but I think we will!"

But here is where our story comes to an abrupt end. It was now Friday, the Inspector and George were in their office when there was a knock on the door. It was the Inspector's old friend, Captain Forth-Right and ex MI 5 officer. "Just popped in old chap. Want a spot of lunch at the club? Now what have we got here?" he said, distracted by the blackboard.

So the Inspector told him about the case. Morris Forth-Right studied the details on the blackboard then said, "Can I use your phone?"

"Of course."

"I would like my ex-boss to see this."

After he put the phone down he said, "Is it okay?"

"Yes."

"Good. He's on his way over right now!"

General Martin Cane was the top man.

"Look sir," Forth-Right said, "look at the names."

"Yes."

"What do you see? Take the first letter going down of each name."

"My God Morris, you may be onto something. BEACH, BEACH, BEACH," the General kept saying. "Richmond was the Pimpernel, that's what we coded him, for he always got away. We could not catch him or know who he was. It was after Richmond closed his shop that by chance we found a letter behind a desk that must have fallen down without him knowing. After he closed down the shop was opened by a blackmarket gang and it was on one of our raids that we found the letter. That was eight months after Richmond gave up the shop. We broke the code or messages with BEACH in them, very clever. So Bell, Evoken, Ackamo, Cho and Hickerman made up the word BEACH but there's a hell of a lot we don't know!"

So for the next six hours they disgussed what they knew and their theories, and by late evening they had a good picture of how the gang worked during the war spying and coding messages back to Germany.

"Was it for the money? Hate for the British?"

"Whatever it was for they almost got away with it. We could not arrest Richmond, there was not enough evidence. So we just trailed him for years, but nothing. So we gave up, until now."

There's a lot of detail I have to miss out for it is still classified top secret and still under Rule B628 Secrets Act, but I can tell you the rest of the story.

A warrant was put out for the arrest of the Richmond Five and a warrant for Alan Richmond, so the police went to the home to be met by Mrs Appleby.

"We have warrants for the arrest of Bell, Evoken, Ackamo, Cho and Hickerman. Could you tell me where they are?"

"Of course. I've noticed them all morning sitting in the garden asleep. Never known that before, mind you it's a hot day. Do they know you were coming?"

"Not sure. Have you seen Mr Richmond?"

"Yes, he's up in his room. He came back last night. He had breakfast with the five then went to his room and he has not come out since."

"What time was this?"

"About 9'o clock."

"Thank you. Have you a key to his room?"

"No he kept it on him all the time..."

"Excuse me sir," George interupted. WBut I think you'd better come into the garden. They are not asleep sir, but all five are dead. I think they all took poison."

"Better call for a doctor, George."

"Right sir."

When the police forced their way into Richmond's room he also was dead. He had left a note only a few words this is what was what it said:

They seek him here, they seek him there,
The five you are seeking are lying out there.

"Well George we will never know the full story, probably not even half of it. But what we've got is six dead bodies!"

"Is that it sir?"

"That's it George."

The following morning the Inspector and George were called to Scotland Yard and were summoned to see . . . guess who? Mr Winston Churchill the Prime Minister.

"The case is closed and so are your lips. Thank you both, I'm recommending promotion for you both. Thank you. Your country thanks you." And with that, cigar in mouth Mr Churchill left the room.

The Inspector's boss said, "The Goodman's files are on your desk Tom. See you Monday."

"Yes sir. Ready, George?"

"Yes sir!"

"Let's go home. Are you hungry George?"

"Starving."

"So am I!"

Points to note

Let's have a look at our story in more detail:

(1) There was a submarine and there was not a submarine   TRUE

(2) Winston Churchill was no fool as the Germans found out

     TRUE

(3) Why, if indeed he did, did Alan Richmond steal the five
   files? Did he not know about the duplicates?
   Did the police or MI5 steal them?   NO ANSWER

(4) Did MI5 know Alan Richmond was the Pimpernel?
     DON'T THINK SO

(5) Was the real Pimpernel living in London all the time and
   not in Liverpool?   DON'T KNOW

(6) Did Alan Richmond kill Dr Zigaman, if so, why?
   We know the doctor was German, MI5 told the police that
   the doctor was also German.   YES

(7) Now, we don't have proof but we think the doctor was
   part of the spy ring and may have wanted out.   YES

(8) We know the five were always together.
   MI5 had broken all the fours spy ring's codes in and around
   Liverpool.   TRUE

(9) Why did the five take poison? Did they know the police were
   on to them?   YES

(10) Why did Alan Richmond also take poison and leave the note?
   Was he teasing the police and he was the Pimpernel?
     DON'T KNOW

(11) Why was a lot of evidence and facts about this case closed
   down by the Government and why did Sir Winston Church
   ill himself get involved and promote the two police officers?

I'll leave it up to you to make up your own mind! Perhaps one day the real story will come out. Was there more to this story than we have been told? Who knows??

One last fact that could give you the answer –

This is what was on the note found by the dead body of Alan Richmond:

They seek him here, they seek him there
The five you are seeking are lying out there.

Walter of Le'Roy County

They say every dog has its day. To some dogs it's a good day to others it's a bad day. To a small town in Texas called Le'Roy it was a . . . well I'll leave you to decide!

It all started June 26th at ten minutes to midnight 1960. Old Orton Ben Pegus, who lost a leg in a truck accident way back in the 1930's, was walking his old sheep dog when he heard the strangest noise he had ever heard. It sounded like a whistle, but half way through the whistle it cut off then started again and it went on and on. To old peg leg Ben, as he was called, it sounded as if it was coming from the doorway of Bert the Butcher's shop.

In the doorway was a cardboard box with a lid on it. Old Ben looked inside the box and there laying in an old bed sheet was a baby. Ben pulled the sheet away from the baby's face, took one look and said aloud, "My God!" He put the lid back on and took the baby to the town police station where a nurse was called in to check the baby out. Tied to the baby's big toe was a tag with a note on it, which read:

WE DON'T WANT HIM HE'S YOURS. HIS NAME IS WALTER DARRANTY WATERS. HE IS TWO WEEKS OLD – TWO WEEKS TOO LONG FOR US!

And that was it. Nothing more. Whoever his parents were they did not want him, so they had dumped him outside the butchers shop door and had ran off.

He was taken to the local children's home while the police tried to find his parents, but they never did. After three months he was put up for adoption. Local people would call to see him with a view to adopt him, but one look at that bundle of noise and they would say, "Thanks, but no thanks," and get away as quickly as possible.

It was said that his parents were an odd couple passing through Le'Roy in an old truck. The local secondhand shop owner remembered them. He said that they had a baby with them that it looked like it was wrapped in an old bed sheet and it kept making a funny whistling sound all the time. The baby's face was covered up.

The shop owner said, "I'd never heard anything like it before, it was doing my brain in. I was glad when they left. They brought a pair of second hand boots for four dollars, then left. I never saw them again that was the late afternoon of the 26th." The next time they were seen was leaving town about 11 o'clock, never to be seen again.

Eventually, when he was just over three months old, old Ma and Pa Bringalstick took baby Walter away from the children's home. Mr Shakky the children's home Superintendent went out and got drunk.

It was sad in a way for as Walter got older his teeth never grew. The town doctor, Dr Frost said, "It happens now and then and it's now!"

But one tooth did grow right in the front top gum of his mouth and it grew wide and long. When he was older he once said, "My gums are so hard I can crack a nut with them!"

Ma and Pa Bringalstick had a small ranch some five miles outside Le'Roy and their own children had all grown up and moved out to live in big cities. Pa Bringalstick was almost deaf and Ma was almost blind but they lived well and got on better than most folk. You always knew if the Bringalsticks and Walter were in town. For if there were any dogs around they would run off with their tails between their legs as fast as they could go, as you could hear that broken whistle sound coming from his throat all the time, from at least twenty yards away.

The doctor said, "I've never heard of it before, but now I have."

He said to another doctor "Perhaps a pea is stuck. What he wants is a punch up the throat!"

When Walter was a year old he looked five years old and when he was five he looked ten and when he was eighteen he looked, well it was anyone's guess, but if you started at fifty and went up you might guess right. The Bringalsticks would not give him their name as they would say, "That's his name he can keep it!" So he stayed Walter Darranty Waters. The town's children gave him a nickname. They called him Dirty Waters as he never washed or shaved and he always wore the same old worn out dirty jeans, old high-heeled cowboy boots and an old cowboy hat. And wherever he went the flies went with him. If he went into a store and there were flies in there, as soon as he walked in all the flies would make a bee line for him and buzz around his head, but it never seemed to bother him one bit. It was said the store owners would call him in so when he went out the flies went out with him and nine times out of ten they did!

He once left town and all the townspeople put in to buy his coach ticket. He said he wanted to see the world, and they were happy to see him go. They even laid on a brass band for him.

But a month later he was back. The station coach manager said, "I've had a funny feeling for the last few days, thousands of flies have been hanging around the coach station. Normally you don't see many!" And when Walter did turn up he was the only one on the coach ... well, that is plus the flies from Montana, Wyoming, Colorado, New Mexico and Elpaso. As soon as he got off the coach the driver drove off at high speed never to return again.

When he got back to the ranch the Bringalsticks had packed up and gone, leaving no new address just a note saying:

> Walter go find a bride,
> And take her to the altar,
> Take a look at Judge Potter's daughter,
> We leave the ranch and all within,
> For what God did to you was surely a sin.
>
> Ma and Pa Bringalstick.

The only person in town who was happy to see Walter was Barber Joe. He was always singing an old hillbilly song that went something like this:

> *You open the door,*
> *The flies swarm in,*
> *You shut the door,*
> *You're sweating again,*
> *Life gets tedious, don't it?*

He knew that when Walter was back in town he would send a message asking Walter to call in on him for a chat. So when Walter did call in, have a chat and leave, so did all the flies in the shop.

Now Judge Potter had one daughter. His wife had had her when she was over fifty years old. They said they don't know how it happened but it did. Mrs Potter was slow if that's the word to use, very slow, let us just leave it at that. The Judge only married her because her daddy had offered a lot of money to whoever married her and as Judge Potter was only training to be a judge, a local one at the time that is, he certainly needed money to finish his training. So one Monday morning at 10'o clock he got himself a wife and ten thousand dollars. But he made sure he was back at his office by 12'o clock and got home that night at 11'o clock, drunk.

The new Mrs Potter was in bed waiting for him, he took one look at her and passed out. That was twenty-five years ago. Judge Potter was now nearly eighty years old, his wife now seventy-five had stopped altogether. And I mean stopped.

Their daughter, well ... she was running on half steam with the breaks on.

So Walter decided to call on Judge Potter's daughter. Her name was Dotty Pots Potter. Pots was her mother's maiden name and she was known to the town's folk as Potty Potter. When Walter got to Judge Potter's house, Potty was sitting at the garden table eating. In one sitting she could eat five home made meat pies, two cow pies, two cherry pies and two plum pies plus a gallon of ale. She could drink any man under the table and she could fight like a bull terrier. When she sat down at the table to eat the Judge and his wife always kept away, if you were to sit at the table at meal times you would see why! She would never use a knife or fork as she would say, "I've got hands that's all I need to eat with!"

If she fell off the chair drunk they left her there to sleep it off. It was anyone's guess at how much she weighed. Put it this way, it took eight men once to carry her into the house, that's why she was left outside most of the time when she was drunk. I'm not saying she was fat, but she made Billy Bunter look like slimmer of the year.

So here was a man of twenty-three; five foot four and six stone three pounds, scruffy, stank, never washed, wore the same clothes week in month out, surrounded by flies wherever he went and every time he breathed it sounded like a broken whistle stuck in his throat, calling on Judge Potter's daughter. Who was, wait for it, six foot four inches tall, weighed around twenty odd stone, whose hobby was eating, eating and more eating. And if you asked her a question make sure that you had plenty of time to wait for an answer. She also wore the same dress all the time, it just hung on her no shape, nothing, and it stopped hanging when it got to her ankles. She had arms like Garth, a pair of hands that would make a rail road navvy look silly and a beam that was a good three foot across. Did I mention her face was…anyway let's move on with our story.

It was love at first sight for both of them. He looked at her and she looked at him and before they knew it they were in love, deep love. It was less than six months from their first meeting that they married. The whole town turned up.

"I wouldn't miss this for anything," Barber Joe said.

The couple lived at the ranch and a year later they had a son called Wapo. How it happened I'll leave it up to you to work out, but if it could happen to Judge Potter's wife at fifty plus then why not to Mr and Mrs Waters? I know it's not the same but there again in a way it is the same. Perhaps with a doctor and like the Beetles, 'With a little help from my friends'. Love is strange, in this case very strange.

But my story has a sad ending. They had only been married three years when while they were out walking one day Potty just dropped dead. They could not find Walter to tell him. It was not until they managed to lift her up from the ground that they found him! She had fallen back, he must have been behind her and tried to catch her and she had fallen on top of him. As they pulled her off of him he gave his last whistle.

And as for baby Wapo, (he was given that name by Judge Potter - the 'Wa' was the first two letters of Walter and the 'po' the first of Pots, so you had Wapo son of Potty and dirty Waters), at two years old Wapo looked like a sumo wrestler. A travelling circus was in town for a week and when they left so did Wapo. Whether he was stolen by the circus people or given to them, who knows. For at that time the bearded lady and a midget had ran off together and the circus may have been looking for something or someone to take their place. The circus' story was they found Wapo in a truck ten miles outside Le'Roy near the monkey house. That's their story and they are sticking to it. The people of Le'Roy are happy to go along with that as long as the circus keeps going and doesn't bring him back. So if you are ever in Texas in a small town called Le'Roy and you see a lot of flies in one place, look out as Walter's ghost may be nearby.

Yakamo

At the turn of the sixteenth century in old Japan in a small village called Nagai lived Nico Samio was a farmer who owned a small farm. Nico Samio had two sons. His first son was called Yakamo. The date of Yakamo's birth is not known. By the time Yakamo was two years old Nico and Mia Samio knew it was going to be a very hard job controlling their son for already at that age he had a very bad and violent temper and if he did not get his own way he made life for Nico and Mia's family very hard.

At three years old he was violent with other children, always wanting to fight them. By the time he was six he was almost out of control for he seemed to have three times the strength of other children his age and would only do what he wanted to and that was to fight anybody.

Day in and day out all he did was look for fights in his village and other villages. By the time he was eight years old he had his own gang who used to go round beating other boys up. It got so bad that the headman of the village said to Nico that he had got to do something with his son or they would have to leave the village. So poor Nico went to see a Samurai who was teaching the sword, archery and horse riding and as luck would have it he got Yakamo enrolled into the school.

Yakamo picked up the sword so fast that he left the other students behind they would keep away from him when training for he would attack as if he was in a real fight. One minute he would be okay, the next he would go into a terrible temper threatening to kill every one. No one could control him.

By the time he was twelve years old he was so good and fast with the sword no one, man or boy, would fight him in training. Yakamo was a violent, rough, powerful and bad tempered young man.

When he was fourteen years old he had mastered the sword, horse riding and archery. He never lost to anybody. He once said, "I was not born to loose, so I will fight anyone to prove it!" And many fights he did have through his lifetime and never lost.

When he was fifteen years old he killed his brother Nico. Yakamo found his brother asleep in his bed. Nico was twenty years old. Yakamo told his brother to get out of his bed, but Nico told Yakamo to go away and let him sleep as he had been working all night on the farm. Yakamo got into a very bad temper, drew his sword and cut off his brother's head. He left the village before any one knew what he had done. He never went back to the village again and he never saw his mother or father again.

No one knows what he did for the next two years he just disappeared. When he was first heard of again was when he killed a man for not getting out of his way. By the time Yakamo was eighteen years old he had a very bad reputation for fighting and killing. He was known for his violent temper that got him into so many fights.

Yakamo lived on his own. He never made friends and moved over the countryside on his own and ate on his own. He hired his sword to anyone who would pay him, it did not matter who they were or why. To him it was just another way of earning money and over the years he hired out his sword many, many times and many fell under it.

He was asked, "Do you like hunting or killing people?"

His answer was, "It is just a job, but a job I love doing."

He soon got the name of Dark Shadow, - you never knew he was there until it was too late as the next minute you would be dead. There are many, many stories about Yakamo.

One story of Yakamo was he walking through the wood when ten bandits jumped out on him. The leader of the bandits said, "Before we kill you and rob you of your clothes and sword we want to know who you are so we know who we have killed!"

Yakamo said, "I am known as Yakamo!"

On hearing this the bandits backed off saying, "Are you the Yakamo they call the Dark Shadow?"

"Yes" he replied.

"We did not know it was you, Yakamo. Go on your way."

But Yakamo said, "No you want to fight so I will fight you all." At that he drew his sword and attacked the ten bandits.

It did not take long before many bandits lay dead and those who had not been killed ran off into the wood.

The leader of the bandits fell to his knees saying, "Don't kill me Yakamo!"

"I will not kill you, you have killed yourself. Stand up, put your arms out straight in front of you."

The bandit leader did as he was told. Yakamo turned as if to walk away then spun round and with one strike cut both arms off of him.

As Yakamo walked away he said, "Yakamo is my name. Take it to your grave for that is the only place that you are going."

Another story is that Yakamo spent the night with a young prostitute. In the morning she asked, "Did I please you master?"

Yakamo said, "No," then cut her throat open.

Robert A Lane

In the next four years Yakamo killed nineteen men by the
sword. Because of his speed and skill no one would fight him
as they knew they were no match for him. But all wanted to kill
him as he was hated everywhere he went. It was said that whenever he turned up in a village or town someone was going to
die.

One day Yakamo was crossing a small bridge when an old
man got in his way.

"Move over old man, for I want to pass!"

The old man said, "I can not move very well or fast as one
of my legs is no good."

Hearing that Yakamo drew his sword and cut off the old
man's bad leg saying, "If your bad leg is no good to you then
you don't need it." And left the old man to bleed to death.

Yakamo once said, "I fear no man. I don't fear death, the
only thing I fear is age for age can bring fear and death."

He was asked, "Have you ever loved someone, do you love
anybody?"

He said, "I love no one for love is the enemy, for love can
kill. Fall and lose your head. I take heads, I do not give mine."

Again he was asked, "Would you change you life if you
could?"

He said, "No. I was made this way by my creator so I must
do what I was made for. When it is my turn to know I will be
told."

Throughout his life Yakamo said, "Killing means nothing to
me, you fight to get into this world so you must fight to stay in
it. Many don't make it into this world and a lot that do don't
stay long. I am two men, one will pick a small baby from the
ground, the other will put a man to the ground."

He was once asked, "Do you have friends?"

He said, "I only have one friend, that friend is the earth, it
gives me water to drink, fruit to eat, stars to light the night, the
sun to warm my body, the air to breathe and smell the flowers,

the earth to make my bed and the birds to sing. None of these are my enemy. Only You!"

It is said that one time when Yakamo was in an eating-house, four men came in drunk. When asked to leave they became abusive to the people in the eating-house. Yakamo told them, "You had better leave."

They left but before they left Yakamo said to them, "Leave while you can hear the music and not feel my sword for the music is loud while my sword is silent. They say the finest wine is your last wine." A Japanese saying meaning 'your life is over.' The next morning four men were found dead and all by the sword.

A wrestler called Kia was a very big and powerful man and had killed four men wrestling before he challenged Yakamo to a wrestling duel saying, "We know how good you are with your sword Yakamo."

"I will fight you Kia," said Yakamo, "if the winner can kill!"

Kia laughed and said, "It will be a pleasure to kill you Yakamo." So the two men wrestled. Kia was performing all his wrestling tricks on Yakamo but Yakomo just kept him off him by using his great strength.

Then when Yakamo was ready he used his great strength to pin down Kia on his front. Yakamo pulled Kia's arms up his back then he broke one arm then the other, then he lifted him up from the ground by the throat with one hand. He held him above his head until Kia was dead, then he threw him to one side like a rag doll. Then he said to the crowd, "All that he had is now yours."

Sometimes Yakamo was not seen or heard of for months at a time. Some said he went up into the mountains to meditate but once he was back you soon knew. There was even a song written about him:

Yakamo's Sword was bright and sharp,
For he killed a pigeon for attacking a lark,
The pigeon turned with a grin, you missed Yakamo try again,
You fool don't you know you're dead
Come on my friend shake your head.

As long as the song told a story it did not matter how the words were written.

Yakamo fought ten thousand men,
And after the battle said, "Let's do it again."

Many people could not get enough of Yakamo and the stories about him. Be the stories true or false it did not matter, they would tell them. Some tales said that Yakamo was the devil come to look at the world some said Yakamo was an old Samurai warrior come back and entered Yakamo's body.

Yakamo's arrows were true and sharp
For he killed an eagle in the dark
The eagle soared the night sky
And Yakamo said, "Its time to die."

One last story about Yakamo. He was challenged by one of the greatest swords men of that time in Japan and for Yakamo to beat this great warrior he would have to be a greater swordsman than the warrior, but he was not. The name of the warrior was Goshi Riosh Ro. But Goshi made one mistake by saying to Yakamo "You can name the place and time." That almost cost him his life.

It was now the month of August. Yakamo sat down to think of a way to beat and kill Goshi Riosh Ro. For three long days he tried hard to think of a way. Then one morning he got his answer. He went to Goshi and said, "I will fight you on the first day of December." Yakamo laughed as he walked away, "I will win fair and square on the day."

Both men agreed and after Yakamo had left Goshi said, "I must rid this earth of such a man for Japan can not hold its head up while such a man walks our land so it will be on the first day of December at 7'o clock in the morning. Yakamo also said, "Our fight will be less than two miles from where we stand." As miles around there was nothing but fields.

Yakamo was now nearly thirty and Goshi Riosh Ro was almost sixty. For the next three months Yakamo could not be found. Some said he had ran from Goshi, others said he had gone away to train. People even went out to try and find him but no one could. Some said he was dead. But on the morning of the last day of November Yakamo turned up at Goshi Riosh Ro's house. "Tomorrow is the first day of December. On that day we fight at 7'o clock in the morning and the place we fight at is in the mid stream of the river Miokka. The water will be waist high. We fight to the death!"

"Agreed," said both men.

Japan in December is bitterly cold. With very cold winds and snow, the water would be freezing, no man would last long in the river.

When Goshi Riosh Ro arrived Yakamo was already in the river - mid stream practising with his sword while waiting for Goshi. Goshi stepped into the water and as soon as he touched the water he knew what the day would bring. He bowed to Yakamo for he knew he was no fool. The fool was him! Yakamo had not cheated, but played the game his way. Goshi went further into the river the water was bitterly cold, by the time he got mid stream, level with Yakamo, Goshi was so cold he could not move his arm above the water. His sword held high but he could not move his arms very fast.

"Ready to fight?" Yakamo shouted.

"We fight and attack!" Goshi said.

Goshi managed to block three strikes from Yakamo. He was now turning blue with cold. He looked at Yakamo and said, "A fair fight. I am ready to die!" And with that he fell back into the water. He was dead, killed by the freezing cold water of the river Miokka.

Yakamo had won but not a drop of blood had been spilt. To Yakamo it was not right, he quickly pulled Goshi out of the river, put warm clothes round him and put him as near as he could to a big fire he had built before the fight. Goshi was blue from tip to toe. Yakamo was also very cold and he had to put on warm clothes and stood by the fire.

"Bring hot wine and food!" he called out. "Try and put wine into Goshi."

Yakamo looked down at Goshi Riosh Ro and said to himself, "Greatest creator of all mankind bring back to life Goshi Riosh Ro and I will never fight again. For I have done him wrong. In the field I would be dead, for I have followed him all the days of my life as he is a true warrior. He is what I always wanted to be."

Because of the bitter cold weather and the freezing water, Goshi had passed out but it seemed his heart was beating very slowly. He appeared dead but was still just alive. Yakamo's action of pulling him out of the water, putting warm clothes on him and laying him by a hot fire, he had saved his life. Very slowly Goshi started to come back to life.

Goshi made a full recovery although it took almost three months. But his days of fighting were over. After they took Goshi home, Yakamo went away and was not heard of for almost a year. Goshi sent his people out to find Yakamo and bring him back.

When he was found, Yakamo went to see Goshi who said, "I have been told of your deeds to me. I live because of you my friend."

That was the first time anybody had called Yakamo friend and meant it.

"I honour you Yakamo for you are a true warrior. To you Yakamo I give my sword, for you alone are worthy of it. From this day on you will be known as Yakamo Ro!"

From that day on a legend was born.

"Also I hear that you do not fight anymore. But as from this day you will only fight for the House Of Goshi Riosh Ro. As you are my warrior, tell me Yakamo how was it you could stand in the cold water and did not nearly die like I did?"

"I went up into the mountains where there is a large and very cold lake. Each day I would go into the lake for a while. I would stay in the lake for as long as possible each day, so by the time I came to fight I could stand in the cold water. I knew that you could not. But I could not beat you on dry land."

Goshi stood up and said to Yakamo.

"You my friend are the true warrior. For yesterday is gone for you. The answers you seek are told today."

Yakamo's words of long ago came true.

"When I am to be told, it will be the right time.
For when I am to know I will be told."

Yakamo lived another thirty-five years and became one of Japan's greatest warriors.